The Trap
Paperback Copyright © 2021 Lorhainne Ekelund

ISBN-13: 9781989698877

Give feedback on the book at:
lorhainneeckhart@hotmail.com

Twitter: @LEckhart
Facebook: AuthorLorhainneEckhart

Printed in the U.S.A

THE TRAP

A BILLY JO MCCABE MYSTERY
BOOK 4

LORHAINNE ECKHART

Lorhainne Eckhart

Roche Harbor looks peaceful from the outside: ocean views, wooded roads, close neighbors, and a small police department where everyone knows everyone. But beneath the surface are missing children, cold cases, corrupt officials, powerful families, and victims no one wants to believe.

Billy Jo knows what it means to be forgotten. A survivor of foster care and childhood trauma, she has built her life around protecting children who have no one else willing to fight for them. She is sharp, guarded, stubborn, and impossible to intimidate—though she often walks straight into danger because she refuses to look away when a child is in trouble.

Mark Friessen knows the law does not always equal justice. A small-town detective with his own failures and regrets, he is trying to do the job right in a place where influence, money, and silence often matter more than truth. He is protective, relentless, and determined to keep his distance from Billy Jo —until every case pulls them closer.

Together, the social worker and the cop uncover what others would rather leave hidden. Each mystery forces them deeper into the island's secrets, where nothing is simple, no one is entirely innocent, and doing the right thing can cost everything.

As Billy Jo and Mark fight for the vulnerable, the missing, and the dead, they also face the one thing neither of them is prepared for: the dangerous pull between them.

Because in Roche Harbor, every secret has a price.

And sooner or later, the truth always comes knocking.

A late-night call. A child in danger. A trap set for the one man who will come looking.

Social worker Billy Jo McCabe knows better than most what happens when a child is left alone in the dark. So when DCFS calls in the middle of the night about an emergency placement, she doesn't hesitate. A girl named Whitney Chandler needs help, and Billy Jo is the one sent to get her.

But the address is wrong. The house is too quiet. And by the time Billy Jo realizes no child is waiting inside, it's too late.

She has been taken.

Detective Mark Friessen knows Billy Jo doesn't disappear. Not without a fight. When her car is found abandoned and a chilling note is left for him, Mark realizes the truth: Billy Jo isn't the target. She's the bait.

The man who took her wants revenge for a case Mark failed

to solve years ago—the disappearance and murder of an Indigenous young woman whose death was buried by broken systems, ignored warnings, and men with too much power to touch.

Now Mark must race against time to find Billy Jo before an old failure becomes a deadly reckoning. But every lead pulls him deeper into a web of lies, offshore property owners, bureaucratic mistakes, and secrets protected by wealth and silence.

And Billy Jo, locked away and running out of time, will have to do what she has always done.

Survive.

A gripping small-town mystery filled with suspense, buried secrets, emotional tension, and a slow-burn connection between a guarded social worker and the detective who refuses to let her go.

CHAPTER ONE

WHAT WAS THAT SOUND?

A distant ringing pulled Billy Jo from a dream. She'd been staring at an arrogant redhead, a man who seemed to look right through her.

She jolted awake. The ringing was her phone, somewhere in the apartment.

Mark Friessen had been in her dreams.

She tossed back the covers, her bare feet hitting the icy floor in the pitch black. Flicking on her bedside light, she hurried out. Her cell phone glowed on the kitchen island.

"Hello?" she said, clearing her throat. The lingering cobwebs of sleep and the phantom anger from Mark's gaze still clung to her. The red digital clock on the stove read 1:10 a.m.

"Ms. McCabe, this is the program director from DCFS. I'm filling in for Grant. I apologize for calling at this late hour, but we have an emergency."

She didn't recognize the voice.

"I'm sorry, who is this?" she asked, shivering as she strode back to her bedroom. Harley, curled half under the covers she'd thrown back, didn't stir.

"Lane Fuller," the man said. "Again, I apologize for the late hour, but a report has come in about a child in trouble. I need you to immediately pick up the child and arrange for emergency placement."

Her hand went to her head, brushing back hair she knew was sticking up everywhere. She grabbed her ratty plush gray housecoat, shrugging one arm in as she hurried back to the kitchen. The bright overhead light flicked on. She blinked, her heart thudding with the familiar warning that always came when she woke in the night.

"What happened?" she asked, spotting her bag. Juggling the phone between her shoulder and ear, she pulled out the pen and notebook she always kept tucked inside. She instinctively rolled her shoulders, feeling the night's chill.

"Not sure on the details. All I know is we're to pick up the kid. The name here is..." The sound he made was cold, unfeeling. She couldn't shake the suspicion that he possessed the familiar trait of too many in this business—a desensitization she'd grown accustomed to, something that seemed to come with the job. Otherwise, it could eat people alive. But she still saw the eyes of all the children, the hope that dimmed there, every night before she slept.

Maybe that was why she felt haunted now.

"Ah, here it is," he said. "Whitney Chandler, and here's the address." He rattled it off, and she scribbled it down, wondering if this job ever got easier.

Billy Jo pressed the pen harder to the paper, already feeling that familiar prickle of irritation. Someone higher up the ladder expected her to run into the dark with half a story and no net.

"Has law enforcement been notified?" she asked.

There was a pause, just long enough for her to hear a faint hiss on the line.

"Not necessary at this point," he said. "This is a placement issue, Ms. McCabe, not a police matter."

She stilled, her pen hovering over the notebook. *Not necessary*. She hated those two words, especially from someone who wouldn't be the one walking up to a stranger's door in the middle of the night.

"And you're sure about that?" she said.

"As I said, this is an emergency placement. We need the child picked up and placed tonight. That's the priority."

Right. The priority. As if the kid were a file to be moved from one desk to another instead of a scared child somewhere in the dark. As if Billy Jo didn't know what happened when people made decisions from behind phones and desks, never once having to look into the eyes of the kid they were talking about.

She wrote *police not called?* in the margin and underlined it.

"And how old is the child? Did something happen? The parents...?"

"I told you this is all I have. It's just an emergency placement. Go get her, find a bed for her tonight, and you can iron out all the details in the morning," he said. Then he hung up. Billy Jo stared at the disconnected phone, glancing at the time again and wondering why emergencies always seemed to happen in the middle of the night.

She hated this. Worse, she hadn't even met the child but could already feel her anguish.

She pulled on thick socks and opted for sweats and a sweatshirt, then ran a brush over her hair, hearing the rain patter on the roof. She reached for her heavy, warm raincoat and shoved her feet into her lined rain boots, then quickly searched up the address. It was a rural, dark part of the island she knew well.

Great, just perfect for a late-night visit.

"Seriously, why does the bad kind of shit have to happen after dark?" she muttered, pissed off. There was something about the night that always had her on edge.

Billy Jo reached for her phone, seeing Mark's name in her contacts, and a wave of unease washed over her. *It was just a dream*, she reminded herself as she thumbed past his name. She opened Pam's contact and dialed, then put it on speaker and listened to it ring once, twice. Then it went to voicemail.

"Dammit, Pam, it's Billy Jo. I need you to get up. I just got a call from some guy filling in for Grant, and I'm doing an emergency placement. There's a kid in trouble. Not sure of the details, but I need you to find a bed for her tonight." She heard the beep and knew she'd been cut off.

She grabbed her bag, then opened the kitchen island drawer for a flashlight. As she strode to the door, phone to her ear, dialing Pam again, she held the notebook open to the address.

"What!"

At least Pam answered this time.

"It's Billy Jo. I just left you a message. Sorry to call in the middle of the night." She pulled open the door and flicked on the outside light. The rain was a heavy, pounding curtain, making everything—seeing, driving, just being out in it—impossible. "I just got a call from the program supervisor. I think he said his name was Lane. I have to pick up a kid in trouble."

She rattled off the address, then tucked the notebook into her coat pocket. Standing in the open doorway, hood up, she stepped out and pulled the door closed, the rain pelting down. "Look, I'm driving out there now, so find a bed if you can. Call me back and let me know where to take her."

Pam's sigh summed up Billy Jo's own feelings. "I'll see

what I can find. Why do these calls always happen in the middle of the night?"

Hadn't she just thought the same thing? She didn't answer, remembering her nights in foster care, lying in the dark. That was when everything bad could and would happen.

"Oh, and Pam, whatever place you find, try to make sure I won't have to worry about pulling this kid from one bad situation and sticking her in another."

"I'll do my best," Pam said.

Billy Jo hung up and tucked the phone in her bag, then made her way down the steps, the rain making everything difficult. She splashed through puddles to her new Nissan, yanked open the door, tossed her bag onto the passenger seat, and climbed in.

She should have brought a towel, water dripping from her. She stared at the outside light, started her car, and let it warm for a second before flicking on the heat and pulling down the darkened driveway to the road.

The wipers whirred on high, battling the rain so hard they couldn't clear it fast enough. Worse, fog had settled in, and she white-knuckled the steering wheel.

"Damn, I hate nights like this," she muttered, struggling to see the faded white lines on the road. The trees pressed in on both sides as she rounded a bend, and she slowed, water splashing under her tires. Turning right, she flicked on her high beams, revealing darkened driveways, some numbered, some not.

"114, where are you?" she repeated, crawling along. Only two driveways displayed numbers. "Sometimes I really hate this island."

She slammed on the brakes, spotting a small white address sign—she'd gone too far. Pulling out her notebook, she found the address and the directions she'd looked up earlier. An uneasy feeling settled in her stomach, a familiar companion on nights like this.

With her foot on the brake, the engine idling, she reached for her phone. One bar. How had it not charged? Had she even plugged it in?

"Stupid, stupid, Billy Jo." She made a rude noise, tapping the phone to her forehead. Frustration coiled with unease. "Come on, keep it together," she muttered, rummaging through her purse. No charger. "Shit! Idiot!"

She slapped the steering wheel, then forced a breath in. Shifting into reverse, she flicked on the rear wipers, backing up until she reached a rutted, tree-lined driveway. This had to be it. She flicked off her high beams as the fog turned the world white, then saw it: a dark house with an older pickup parked out front.

She gripped the steering wheel, studying the small, two-story house. A light glowed upstairs. She'd expected someone to be here already.

The police? Mark. The thought brought a familiar pang. Arrogant, unhealthy for her well-being, she reminded herself.

Yet, in that moment, she would have given almost anything to see the flash of his red hair in the dark, the broad set of his shoulders, that arrogant cop stance that annoyed her as much as it steadied something inside her.

Which was exactly the problem.

She tightened her hands on the steering wheel, looking away from the house. No police cruiser. No Mark. No one.

Just her, the rain, a dead stretch of road, and a house that didn't feel right.

The dream had been a reminder that she was depending on him in ways that would end up breaking her.

She turned off her car and picked up her phone. When she tried to call Pam again, the screen flashed from one bar to no service. She lifted it, moving it until a single bar reappeared, then pulled up Mark's number and typed a quick text: *Got a call to pick up a kid in trouble. Wondering if you received anything? Here now, but no one else is...*

Her thumb hovered over the send button. She wanted to kick herself for doing exactly what she shouldn't. "Nope, nope, not happening," she muttered, deleting the message. The battery was now in the red.

"This is just great, Billy Jo," she said under her breath. "Pam can't even call you now to let you know where to take the kid, and where are you but in between Crazytown and Creepyville?"

She opened her door, gave it a shove, and reached for the flashlight in her purse. Stepping out, her foot landed squarely in a puddle, the rain still pouring down. She closed the door, flicked on the flashlight, and watched her breath fog in the beam as she started past the truck toward the three wide steps leading to the front door. Solid wood, no doorbell.

Her hand was wet and cold. She fisted it to knock, feeling the hair rise on the back of her neck, that same sick feeling she'd had as a kid, when everything always went from bad to worse. It was the strange doors she remembered so vividly: old, worn, dirty, marked up or scraped and patched.

Some houses smelled of old carpet and cigarettes, of grease left too long in a pan, of damp clothes piled somewhere no one wanted to deal with. Some had porch lights that didn't work, and windows covered from the inside, as if whatever happened in those houses needed to stay hidden. Some had men behind them who smiled too much, women who looked away too fast, and kids who learned early that crying only made things worse.

She could still feel that little-girl part of herself standing on those porches with a garbage bag of clothes at her feet, waiting for someone to decide whether she was worth letting in.

Strange doors always took something from you before they opened.

Billy Jo forced her hand into a fist and knocked anyway.

No one was around. The rain was the only sound she heard as she pictured her uncharged cell phone in the car. Then she knocked again, and this time she knew someone was on the other side of the door. It was just a feeling.

"Hello? Can you open the door, please? My name is Billy Jo McCabe, with DCFS. We got a call about..."

She heard the click of the door unlocking, then the squeak as it opened. A faint light appeared on the other side, followed by the clang of metal. She focused everything on that sound—a gun being cocked, a sound she knew too well. Staring in horror, seeing everything and nothing, she reminded herself to breathe.

"Well, then I guess you'd better come in," a raspy voice said.

The icy chill that ricocheted through her brought a sudden, stark realization: she was alone, with no backup, no help. Staring at the steel of the gun and the pale hand holding it, she knew, whatever this was, she was in over her head.

CHAPTER TWO

"MARK, PAM HUNT IS ON THE LINE FOR YOU." GAIL gestured toward him with the phone. Her bulky purse was already packed and resting on her desk—a sure sign she was ready to leave and the chief was likely two steps from opening the door. Gail stood behind her desk, placing the black office phone back in its cradle, her gaze pointed in that motherly way of hers.

Mark walked back to his desk, holding his steaming coffee, still expecting the chief any second. "Pam Hunt... Should I know who that is?" He glanced at the clock; it was almost ten. Great. This would be a really long day with the chief. The dread was a familiar companion; they'd been circling each other like dogs.

"Pam, who runs the DCFS office here. Come on, Mark, you should know her. Doesn't she work with your girlfriend?"

He wasn't sure what expression crossed his face. Gail was already looking away, pulling a compact from her bag and sliding lipstick over her lips. "Billy Jo is not my girlfriend," he said. "We're friends. That's it. Why do I have to keep telling everyone?"

There it was, the flash of humor in her light blue eyes. She pressed her lips together, giving him that odd smile as she tossed her lipstick and compact back into her bag. Again, she flicked him that motherly look. "Lighten up, Mark. Just having fun at your expense."

He only shook his head and reached for the phone. Why would Pam be calling him? As he held the receiver, he watched the blinking light of the line. "She asked for me by name?"

"Yes, Mark, she asked for you. That's why she's waiting there on hold and why I said she's on the phone for you. So why don't you pick up and ask her nicely what you can help her with? You know, be the good cop you're supposed to be— helpful, community-minded..." Her tone dripped with sarcasm.

He glanced at Carmen's empty desk. He hadn't seen her this morning, which was unusual. He pressed the button on the office phone, picking it up, unsure if he'd ever had a conversation with Pam. "Detective Friessen," he said, keeping his tone even.

"Hi, Detective, this is Pam Hunt. I don't know if you remember me. I work with Billy Jo, and I'm wondering if maybe you've heard from her...last night or this morning?"

He couldn't quite place the edge in her voice. He thought about the last time he'd seen Billy Jo, walking out of the post office days ago. She'd ducked her head, and he'd kept walking. Evidently, they were back to that again.

"Not recently. Why, what's up?" He took a swallow of coffee, watching Gail tuck files from the cabinet behind her into her bag. Case files? One folder sat crooked against the side of her purse, the tab sticking up just enough for him to catch part of the label.

Brown.

He didn't know why the name snagged his attention. Gail

had no business taking case files home unless the chief had told her to. Then again, the chief and Gail had their own way of doing things, and Mark had learned quickly that asking questions in that office usually earned him more silence than answers.

"Well, I haven't seen her this morning. She was supposed to pick up a girl last night, a late-night call, but this morning I got a call from the Pearsons, the placement home, and they said they waited up all night and no one showed up. And she's not answering her cell phone."

The coffee suddenly tasted wrong. Too bitter, too hot, sitting in his throat as if he'd swallowed something he shouldn't have. He lowered the mug, feeling the heat against his palm, and stared at the blinking light on the phone.

Gail had her keys in hand and had lifted her bag over her shoulder. He wanted to know what files she was taking. Maybe the chief had asked her to bring them home? Maybe it was nothing. Maybe Billy Jo not showing up was nothing too.

Except Billy Jo didn't strike him as the kind of woman who forgot a kid, forgot a placement, forgot to call.

"I'm sure there's an explanation," he said. "A late-night call... Maybe she went back to bed. Maybe there wasn't an issue after all. I'll try her cell phone, but it's likely she's sleeping."

"Look, I've called her cell phone four times," Pam said. "If she was answering, I wouldn't be calling you now, would I? This isn't like her. She's had late-night calls before, but she's always first here. She said she'd been told to pick up a girl. She'd have left me a message if something had changed."

He pulled in a breath, knowing he'd have to drive over to her place. He'd have to talk to her. He could already imagine the awkwardness that lingered between them now, because he knew her better than any woman he'd ever known. Sharing, talking... She knew too many secrets he didn't share with anyone.

"I'll call her, then drive over to her place," he said. "She'll likely be pissed because I woke her up."

He heard the sigh on the other end of the phone. "Well, tell her to call me, because I have to call the Pearsons back about whether to expect the girl she was supposed to drop off. They aren't happy. No, scratch that. They're furious, actually, and are on my ass, ready to take a chunk out, so to speak. You know what I mean? It's hard enough to find people ready and willing to take a kid in on a moment's notice..."

He didn't miss the sharpness in her tone. He lifted his gaze to the ceiling, wondering how her worry had suddenly turned into a rant. "I hear what you're saying, Pam, but I'm sure it's—"

"What? That she forgot to call, or was it something else?" She cut him off as if she were scolding him.

He was well aware that forgetting to call back was something Billy Jo didn't do. Before he could add anything, Pam continued.

"You just let her know that Jill Pearson waited up all night after I called and told her a girl was being dropped off. She's tired and angry. Billy Jo can call her back and explain and smooth it over with her, because I won't."

It wasn't lost on him how quickly her worry had changed to annoyance. "I will let her know. Anything else?"

There was silence for a second. "I think that's all—other than to let her know that when she doesn't show up in the morning, I'm the one who has to field questions and calls with no answers to give, and I don't appreciate it."

He only nodded, figuring Pam could go on and on. "Duly noted, Pam. I'm sure Billy Jo didn't go out of her way to make things difficult for you. How about I just go over to her place and let her know she needs to talk to you, and then the two of you can work this out?"

He could feel Gail watching him, but he didn't look over. Silence hummed on the other end of the line. "Anything else I can do for you, Pam?" he finally asked, keeping his tone professional, wondering for only a second what was truly going on between the two women. The last thing he wanted was to step into it.

"I think that's all. Just—"

"Okay, Pam. The quicker I get out to Billy Jo's and get you two back in touch, the quicker she can handle whatever needs to be handled," he said, then hung up before she could add one more thing.

"What's going on? Problem?" Gail asked. Did she have any idea Pam could go on and on?

Just then, the front door opened and the chief walked in. Mark yanked open his drawer, pulled out his Jeep keys, then glanced down at the dog he still hadn't named, who was curled up on the dog bed Gail had picked up.

"Billy Jo hasn't checked in this morning. Pam's short version is she had a late-night call to pick up a girl who was supposed to be taken to some foster place, but she didn't show. So, I'm heading over to her place. I'll knock. She's probably asleep. Maybe it wasn't the situation she expected, and if she was up most of the night, it's likely she and Pam got their wires crossed. Come on, dog," he called out.

Across the room, the chief stared at him with that hard, unsmiling gaze, those icy blue eyes Mark knew carried a world of secrets, the kind he didn't want to get too close to. He just waited, feeling as if something was coming. The dog nudged his side, and he found himself looking back at Gail, who only nodded as she slid her hand over the strap of her bag.

The file labeled Brown was gone now, swallowed by the

oversized purse at her side. She adjusted the strap as if there was nothing unusual about walking out of a police station with case files tucked beside her lipstick and keys.

"Well, you'd better get going," was all she said.

The chief didn't pull his gaze from Mark, but he did step back and drawl, "When you're back from your errand, Mark, I need you here, manning the phones." He was a big man, and for a moment Mark could feel the tension that would likely always be there.

"Tolly, you have your own work to do and a number of messages on your desk," Gail said, gesturing.

The chief dragged his gaze to Mark, then stepped back. Mark walked past him and pulled the door open. The dog trotted out ahead. Mark glanced back at Gail and the chief, a silent tension hanging between them—something he definitely didn't want to unravel.

"I'll be back as soon as I can," he said, pulling the door closed behind him. He started for his Jeep, a knot tightening in his gut. This stalemate with the chief, he sensed, was only headed from bad to worse.

CHAPTER THREE

BILLY JO'S CAR WASN'T AT HER PLACE.

Mark rolled down the Jeep's windows. "Stay," he told the dog, who sat patiently in the passenger seat, then closed the door. He scanned the apartment above the garage. In the distance, the Lancasters' large house sat nestled among trees and grass. Everything looked quiet.

He pulled out his phone and dialed Billy Jo's number, wondering if he'd simply missed her. Likely, he was on a wild goose chase, but at least it had gotten him out of the office and away from the chief.

The call went straight to voicemail: "This is Billy Jo McCabe, with DCFS. If this is an emergency, call the office. Otherwise, leave a message and I'll get back to you."

"Hey, I'm outside your place," he said. "Can you call me back as soon as you get this? Pam called, looking for you, so here I am, doing my due diligence, checking up on you. I'm figuring you're likely already at the office and have sorted out this mess with Pam. But call me back and let me know so I can take this off my plate."

He hung up, figuring she'd either call back or ignore him. When had things become so awkward?

Then he spotted someone walking his way, waving. It was Lesley, the owner of the property, a little heavyset in yoga pants and a tank top.

"Yoo-hoo, hey there!" she called out, a happy singsong in her voice. He could hear her smile before he saw it as she hurried over. "Detective, isn't it?"

They'd met a few times, and from the vibes she gave off, he was positive she had no boundaries.

"Yes, Mark Friessen," he said.

"That's right, you're Billy Jo's detective friend. I saw you pull in and wondered who was coming up. Billy Jo isn't here. Is she expecting you? That girl's an early bird. Lorne said he heard her pull out last night during that downpour, in the wee hours, I think. I was planning on bringing some muffins down. When I looked out while making coffee, she was already gone. That girl works so hard, so dedicated. We like her."

Right. Lesley could go on and on.

"You said she pulled out last night," he prompted. "What time did she come back?"

Lesley's bright smile, revealing crooked lower teeth, faded into a frown as she looked up at Billy Jo's place. "I don't rightly know. It had to have been early because, as I said, her car was gone when I got up. Is something wrong? Did you two get your wires crossed?"

Her perceptiveness wasn't lost on him. The way she'd asked that last part held a hidden meaning he didn't want to delve into.

Mark inhaled. "She's not at the office. That's why I'm here. And no, I haven't talked to her."

Lesley frowned again, then opened her mouth to speak. Her gaze drifted to the apartment, to the closed door, and she took in the quiet around them. "Well, did you try calling her?"

"Wouldn't be here if she'd answered. Goes right to voicemail."

Lesley waved a dismissive hand. "Oh, that girl always forgets to charge her phone—or is there something I should be worried about? You two are talking, right?" She winked, a flirty smile touching her lips. What was it with everyone sticking their noses into his business?

Mark glanced at the stairs. "I haven't talked to her in a while. A call came into the station this morning, looking for her. That's why I'm here, just to make sure everything is okay."

Lesley's smile vanished. "You're thinking something's happened to her?"

He shook his head. "Don't know. That's why I'm out here. You mind if I go up and have a look inside?"

She hesitated, and he braced himself for a refusal. "Well, you are a friend. I suppose it'll be all right. I'll get the key." She turned and called out to the man pushing a wheelbarrow in front of the big house. "Lorne, bring the key down for the apartment!"

Mark's foot hit the first step as the man yelled back, "What for?"

"Just bring it! The detective here, he needs to get in," she yelled, her voice carrying easily.

He took in the big window. A three-legged cat jumped to the sill, meowing. He cupped a hand over his eyes, peering past the sun's glare through the glass, but saw no one—just the cat.

As he stepped back, Lesley waved at her husband at the foot of the stairs, urging him to hurry. Mark put his hand on the knob and turned. The door opened. Apparently, his little talk with Billy Jo about locking her door hadn't sunk in.

"Forget the key," he said. "She left the door open." He stepped inside as the cat meowed and hopped across the floor. "Billy Jo, it's Mark," he called, but heard nothing, already knowing she wasn't there.

He scanned the neat and tidy counter. Her charger was still plugged into the kitchen outlet, the cord dangling uselessly beside the island. No phone. No bag. No Billy Jo.

"Damn it," he muttered, picturing her calling herself stupid for leaving it behind.

The cat hopped to the kitchen, where his water bowl lay on its side, empty. His food dish held only a few kibbles.

"You thirsty, hungry? Where's Billy Jo?" he asked the cat, then leaned down, lifted the bowl, and walked to the sink to fill it.

"She left the door unlocked?"

He glanced over his shoulder to see Lesley walk in, her husband following. Lorne's hair was salt and pepper, and he was of medium height, a little on the heavy side.

"What's going on?" Lorne asked, looking around, a frown knitting his brow. "Did something happen to Billy Jo?"

Mark settled the bowl of water on the floor for Harley. "Do you know where Billy Jo keeps the cat food? I think he's hungry." He gestured to the cat, who was already at his water dish.

Lesley made her way into the small kitchen, opened a cupboard, and pulled out a container. "Are you hungry there, you poor little misfit?" she cooed, fussing over the cat.

Mark strode out of the small, open kitchen and down the hall, stopping in her bedroom. Blankets and sheets were tossed back, as if she'd just climbed out of bed and left. He didn't know if she was the kind of girl who made her bed or just got up and went, but given how neat everything else in the place was, he suspected she did—unless she was rushing out in the middle of the night.

He flicked on the bathroom light, revealing the usual toiletries, hairbrush, toothbrush, and towels. Nothing seemed out of place. When he strode back into the living room, Lesley had fed the cat, and Lorne stood with his arms crossed.

"Nothing seems out of place here," he said. Maybe she was still at the call she'd gotten the night before. He pulled out his phone and dialed her office.

"Family Services. This is Pam."

"Hey, it's Mark. Has Billy Jo shown up at the office? I'm at her house, and she isn't here."

"No, she hasn't. I take it you haven't found her?"

He shook his head, his gaze lifting to the Lancasters, who were quietly listening. "Nope. I'm at her place now, and it looks like she left in a hurry. Where did you say she went, again? I think you'd better give me all the details—the name, the address. She could still be out there. Maybe there's more going on than you know. How long ago did you speak to her?" He heard a sigh on the other end.

"She called me in the middle of the night. I think it was after one a.m., maybe closer to two?"

He dragged his gaze to the clock on the stove. It was 11:20 a.m. That familiar, uneasy feeling settled in his gut. "Okay, and you haven't seen her, and you know for sure she didn't go into the office, even before you got there?"

"Look, she wasn't here. I'm in at eight, but this morning I came in early, just after seven, because there's always a lot to do when a kid is picked up the night before. Emergency placements are just that. Then there are the reports and the matter of finding something permanent. No one has any idea of the amount of paper and details that—"

"Okay, I get it," he cut in, realizing Pam could quickly stray into unhelpful topics. "But right now, I'm trying to find out where Billy Jo is, so tell me who she went to see—the name, the address, and the reason she went out there. I'll start there. As I said, maybe she's still there." He heard rustling on the other end, maybe paper.

"She called me, as I said, between one and two. Said she got a call from the program supervisor to pick up a girl by the name of..." She paused. "Here it is. Her name is Whitney Chandler. No other details. Do you want the address?"

"Text it to me at this number." He looked over at Lesley and Lorne, seeing their worry.

"Okay, sending it to you now," Pam said.

"All right. I'll call you if there's anything else," he said, then hung up before Pam could add something. His phone dinged, and there was the address—another rural spot on the island, just what he loved.

"Should we be worried? Should we call her parents?" Lesley said.

Mark looked over at the couple and shook his head. "No sense worrying them. I'm sure wires were just crossed, and Billy Jo is still at the home. I'll drive out there. Don't worry. She'll likely be back here soon. In case she shows up before I find her, though, give me a call." He reached into the breast pocket of his jean jacket and pulled out a card, which he held out to Lorne.

"Sure, we'll call. But if she is out there, let us know. Because now we're worried," Lesley added, taking the card.

Mark merely nodded and glanced down at the cat, now eating. He walked to the door. "Oh, again, don't call Chase and Rose McCabe. If I've learned anything, you'll likely be jumping the gun, and then Billy Jo will have a worried father and mother on the next ferry over."

The way they looked at each other, though, Mark had a feeling that as soon as he walked out the door, Lesley would be on the phone to Billy Jo's parents.

There was one thing he knew well about Billy Jo: she

loved her family, but she was about as private as they came. Having a bunch of people fussing and showing up worried about her was exactly what she wouldn't want.

He strode down the stairs, seeing the dog hanging its head out the Jeep window as he started toward it. This feeling, the one that settled deep in his gut, had him wondering whether he had become too close to Billy Jo, fast treading into that territory where he was beginning to care too much for her.

"Yeah, your judgment's clouded. That's all, Friessen. Pull your head out of your ass and do your job. Treat her like anyone else," he said out loud as he yanked open the door.

But her image popped into his mind again—the last time he'd seen her, with that smile she rarely offered, the awkwardness that had become too real. He had never pictured her as the kind of girl who would eventually shred his heart.

CHAPTER FOUR

"Hello?" Billy Jo yelled, pounding the metal wall, hearing it rattle. Very little light filtered into the room from cracks in the walls as she kept pounding, with no clue where she was.

What had happened after she woke up on the floor of this dark room? It was fuzzy, but she knew there had been a gun, a man. She was in trouble.

"Hey, I know you're out there! Open up! What do you want? Look, I'm not sure who you are, but I got a call to come out here and pick up Whitney Chandler, a young girl who's in trouble. Is she out there? Hello?" she yelled again, banging with her fist. But no one answered.

She was sweating in her heavy raincoat and track pants. Shrugging off her coat, she felt the small flashlight and her extra keys in her pocket. She pulled out the flashlight, flicked it on, and tossed her raincoat to the ground. She was inside what looked like a metal cargo container. She knew cargo containers, but she had no idea where she was. Where were her bag and her cell phone, which wasn't even charged?

"Idiot," she muttered, remembering her car, the rain, and where she'd left her bag and phone the night before.

She closed her eyes for a second, thinking of the text she should have sent Mark. But why would she have done that when she was furious with him? And over what? Her ego, her own issues—because he'd found a way under her skin, grown too close. Now it seemed ridiculous, and she was already kicking herself. Still, she had told Pam where she was, and that program director, Lane, who'd said he was filling in for Grant. That didn't exactly leave her with a warm and fuzzy feeling, though.

"Pam, please tell me you've got this handled, that you've figured out I'm in trouble and called in the cavalry." Her words echoed in the empty container.

Where was she, exactly? She couldn't remember anything past having the gun in her face and then waking up in this box. Why was there a big blank? She tapped her forehead with her fist, struggling to remember.

She was hungry, and she needed to pee. She shone her flashlight around the box, empty except for her. No chair, no crate, no forgotten tool—nothing she could use as a weapon except the flashlight and her keys. She ran her palm along the wall, feeling for a screw, a lip of metal, anything that could cut rope or skin or give her a way out. Nothing. Just cold steel, rust that flaked under her fingers, and one place near the bottom where daylight came in, thin as a blade.

She crouched, holding the flashlight close to the floor, following that line of light. Dirt had blown in along the seam. So had a dead fly and a few bits of straw. Straw meant a barn maybe, or a shed, or some old outbuilding. She pressed her ear to the wall and held her breath, listening.

Nothing.

No cars. No voices. Not even birds, just the hollow sound

of her own breathing and the faint tick of metal settling around her.

She walked to the door and pushed on it. Of course, it was locked, so she kicked it with her booted foot. The rattle was loud, and there was no give.

"Hey, knock it off in there!"

She heard the voice—the same male twang that had accompanied the gun in her face. It had to be the same voice. Everything had gone into slow motion when she heard the click of metal, the long pull of her breath, the icy fear that scraped through her, seeing the barrel in her face.

The door unlocked with a heavy clang. A cargo container, for sure. She flicked off the flashlight and shoved it down the side of her bulky boot, then took a step back, and another. Only one of the doors swung open, revealing a man with dark, shoulder-length hair in need of a cut, and a beard. He was big, likely close to six feet. Something about the way his dark eyes looked at her reminded her of Mr. Humbolt, one of her foster parents, a man who'd loved his guns. Her father, Chase McCabe, had saved her from him. Maybe that was why her heart hammered in her chest.

He smelled faintly of motor oil and damp wool, as if he'd been working around machinery or old trucks. When he reached up to push his hair from his face, his sleeve rode back, and she caught a glimpse of dark ink winding over his forearm. A bear, maybe. Or a wolf. Something with teeth.

"What do you want with me? And where's Whitney? Who the hell are you?" she demanded. She sounded confident, damn it, even though she was shaking inside, fighting the instincts of a scared little girl, alone with no one to help her.

The man had big hands. He gestured for her to move back, then rested a bucket in the corner and tossed a plastic bag on the floor.

"Look, I don't know what this is, but let me out," she said. "I'm Billy Jo McCabe, with DCFS. I don't know what your problem is, but let me see Whitney. Is she all right? What do you want with me? And who are you?" She rested her hands on her hips, mainly because she couldn't stop them from shaking.

"You ask a lot of questions, and you're making too much noise," he said.

Behind him, she could see sunlight through cracks in a wooden wall. A barn, or maybe a big shed? She couldn't be sure.

"You haven't answered me," she said. "Who are you? Where's Whitney? You know keeping me here isn't going to work out well for you. You think people don't know I'm here? My boss, the police..."

There was a smile, she thought. Then it was gone. He didn't pull his gaze, and those eyes were freaking her out, because they held the kind of hate and anger she knew meant he wouldn't be reasoned with.

"Oh, I'm counting on that," he said. "But if you don't quiet down, I'll tie you up and gag you. Are we clear?"

What the hell was that supposed to mean?

He gestured to the bag. "Water and a sandwich." Then he stepped back, his hand on the door. She knew he was about to shut and lock it, so she hurried to it and slapped her hand on it.

"Wait! Who are you? What do you want with me?"

He stopped. The way his gaze lingered on her sent a shiver through her. Anger, rage... He didn't seem inclined to answer. He simply pulled the gun from the small of his back, from the waistband of his jeans, and flicked it at her. "Back," he snapped, gesturing with it.

She lifted her hands and took a step, knowing as soon as

that door closed, there would be no way out. "Please, why? Just answer me that."

"You're a means to an end."

She wondered if her confusion showed. "I don't know who you are, but you know me?"

He still held the gun on her, his finger resting at the side of the trigger, like a pro. "Oh, I know who you are, Billy Jo McCabe. Asked around, and it seems you're as new to the island as Detective Friessen."

She was never at a loss for words, but for a moment, she felt as if she'd been pulled into a game without knowing any of the rules. "Okay, and you have an issue with me...?" She let the question hang, acutely aware of the steel door that would close and lock any second.

He didn't look away. "Didn't say it was about you, now, did I? Just that I know who you are. You know anything about hunting?"

That was exactly what she didn't want to hear from someone holding a gun.

"Some. Why? What is this?"

"Then you know you have to track your prey. You have to wait, and you have to be patient, knowing it takes as long as it's going to take. Sometimes you need bait that will attract who you're hunting. You're my bait."

He was serious. She realized his anger wasn't for her; she was just collateral, staring into the eyes of a man who wouldn't lose a moment's sleep if he pulled the trigger and shot her.

"This is about Detective Friessen?" she said. The man's steady stare told her she was right.

"We have unfinished business," was all he said.

Her stomach knotted as she pictured a trap being set for a man she realized she cared far too much for. She needed to keep this guy talking.

"Well, then you have the wrong person. I'm just a social worker. I barely know him..."

He laughed and shook his head. "Really? You think I didn't do my homework? I know exactly who Mark Friessen is close to on this island, which cabin he lives in, which dog he took in. You're the one he cares for, whether as friends or something more. The talk in town is about the social worker and the cop, and the fact that he'd do anything for you. A man doesn't do that for a woman he barely knows. He does it for a woman he loves. I'd say that makes you the perfect bait."

What the hell? How was this possible—a stranger knowing all this about her and Mark? Who was he?

"You still haven't told me who you are. What's your name? What are you planning on doing to the detective?"

"You ask a lot of questions. It doesn't matter who I am. All that matters is I have you. The detective and I have some unfinished business, and I plan to make him look me in the eye, to hold him accountable. Retribution... I've waited a long time, and I'll have it."

So she was only a pawn. "What did he do?"

He shook his head. "I think the question is what he didn't do." He tucked the gun into his waistband and moved his hand to the door to shut it.

"There is no Whitney, is there?"

He made a face and shook his head. "Nope, not anymore."

CHAPTER FIVE

Mark pulled up in front of an old two-story house, taking in the dirt driveway and overgrown grass, the rutted tire tracks now dry after the heavy rain from the night before. The clapboard siding looked more like an amateur project than something done by a builder, and an old truck sat parked out front. The porch had three wide wooden steps, no railing, and wood that looked as if it had seen better days.

"You stay," he told the dog, whose window was down, already panting as the day warmed. The dog was the best companion he'd ever had.

He stepped out of his Jeep and closed the door, his hand resting on the open window frame. The house windows were single-paned and dirty. An old sheet, he thought, hung in one. He turned his head, seeing trees, overgrown grass, and bushes, but he heard nothing other than birds.

It was deserted and quiet. Too quiet.

He walked around the front of the Jeep and took in the old truck, which didn't look as if it even ran, let alone had moved in a while. The side was rusty, the seat inside was torn, and one of the tires was flat. He patted it, and the sound echoed.

A breeze picked up, and Mark pulled off his sunglasses, tucking them into his shirtfront. Each creak of the wooden steps echoed under his weight. Sweat slicked his back beneath his jean jacket. This place left him with an unsettled feeling, an urge to glance over his shoulder.

His gaze returned to the old wooden door—no doorbell, just scraped, dinged, and dirty wood. He fisted his hand, knocked, and waited, listening. One, two... he counted, then knocked again, louder. "Roche Harbor Police! Open up!" he called.

If anyone was inside, they would have heard him. Yet, there was no sign of Billy Jo or her car. Was this even the right place? Perhaps the address was wrong.

The unsettling sensation persisted. The hair on his neck stood on end, and he turned, narrowing his gaze, unable to shake the feeling of being watched. But he saw only trees and bushes.

"Hey!" he called, expecting someone to emerge, but there was nothing except his dog, head out the open window, panting, loyal and patient.

Mark turned back to the door. Silence. He reached for the knob. It turned, but the door was locked.

He strode down the steps, his holstered gun a familiar weight at his side, and walked to the side of the house, scanning the second-story windows. Around back, the overgrown grass appeared undisturbed. He took in the small, box-like back porch, an old door, and dirty glass.

Behind him, what looked like junk lay scattered. He fanned a hand over his eyes, looked up, then pulled his phone from his pocket and dialed Pam. Clearly, he was missing something.

"DCFS. Can I help you?"

"Pam, it's Mark. I'm at that address you gave me, but it's a rundown old place, deserted. Billy Jo's car isn't here either. Are you sure you gave me the right address? I need you to tell me again exactly what Billy Jo said when she called you."

A pause, then Pam rattled off the same address. Mark nodded to himself, a sinking feeling in his gut.

"Are you sure that's the one she gave you?"

"Look, it may have been the middle of the night, but it's what she told me. I wrote it down. Maybe she gave the wrong address."

Something about this place still didn't sit right.

"Who called her, again?" he asked. He could hear papers rustling in the background.

"The program supervisor. She said his name was Lorne—or Lane, I think? Shit, I know I wrote it down here somewhere..."

He waited, rubbing the back of his neck, no longer feeling that odd sense of being watched.

"Okay, maybe I didn't," she said. "Just the program supervisor. I guess Grant must be away. I'll call his office and find out who called her. Likely it's just the wrong address or something, but that still doesn't explain why she hasn't called or shown up with Whitney..."

It was the "or something" that worried him. The unease he hadn't felt before was starting to sink in. Maybe he should call Billy Jo's dad, her mom? Or maybe there was a simple explanation for all this.

"You know what?" he said. "Call whoever called her. Find out who it was, and I want to talk to him. What did you say the reason was? If a girl was in trouble, why weren't we called? I have no report from last night. Don't you think that's rather odd?"

Silence stretched on the other end. "I guess I never considered that, but the police aren't always involved," Pam said. "Evidently, I don't have the whole story. Do you think something happened, on this island, in our community?"

He heard the doubt—but what was she expecting him to say, that nothing could happen here? Of course it could, and it did. Most people had no idea what went on right next door, not really.

"Don't start speculating," he said. "One thing at a time. I want to talk to the program supervisor, and I need the details of the call, the correct address, and to know why we weren't contacted. Better yet, send me the number of whoever called her, because I want to talk to him. I want all the details of what Billy Jo was sent into."

"Yeah, of course," Pam said before she hung up.

Mark thumbed through his phone and sent a quick text to Carmen: *Where are you?*

Maybe she had an idea of what had happened, considering he hadn't seen her that morning, which was unusual in itself.

Busy, handling something. What do you want? she texted back.

Okay, so she was her usual self.

Looking for Billy Jo. You haven't heard from her, have you?

He waited for the three dots, watched them pop up as if she was typing, but then there was nothing. He lifted his gaze, scanning the junk-filled yard, and took a step toward what looked like a kitchen window. He glanced back at his cell phone. The message: Nope.

That was it.

He shook his head, tucking his cell into his back pocket. He looked up at the kitchen window again, then at an old barrel and pallets leaning against the house. He dragged one under the window, testing it with a booted foot before climbing up. Pressing his hands against the

wall, he cupped one against the dirty window and peered in. An empty kitchen. Paper and boxes scattered on the floor.

Cupboard doors hanging open. A dusty, dirty pot sat on an old stove. Abandoned, maybe.

He jumped down, pulled out his phone, and sent another text to Carmen. *Can you pull up this address for me? Looks abandoned. Find out who owns it, who lives here, everything.*

A thumbs-up emoji appeared, and he tucked his phone back into his pocket, striding around the house. When his Jeep came into view, he froze. Something white fluttered under his wiper blade.

"What the hell...?"

He slapped his hand to his side, reaching for his gun as he stared at the paper. It hadn't been there before. As he moved closer to the side of the house, looking around, the feeling of being watched returned, making the hair on his neck prickle.

He drew a breath, his heart pounding. He took one step, then another, staying close to the house, his hand on his gun, tracking everything as he glanced around the corner. Nothing. He knelt, peering under the Jeep. Still nothing—no feet, no one.

He hurried over and snatched the paper. Someone had put it there while he was behind the house. Someone was watching him.

Worse, someone had been close enough to his Jeep to tuck a note under his wiper. He was a cop. He should have heard something, seen something, felt the shift in the air before whoever it was got that close.

He hadn't.

The shame of it hit fast and hot, right under his ribs. If he'd missed this, what else had he missed? Billy Jo's car. Billy Jo herself. Whatever trap she had walked into because someone had known exactly how to pull her out into the dark.

Then he realized. The dog hadn't barked. He glanced inside.

The passenger seat still held the dent of his body, and a long smear of drool marked the inside of the door.

But the dog was gone.

No bark. No growl. No warning.

"Dog?" Mark called, keeping his voice low, though everything in him wanted to shout. He stepped back, sweeping his gaze over the trees, the porch, the old truck, the shoulder of the road. "Come here."

Nothing.

No jingle of a collar. No rush of paws through grass. Just the paper snapping lightly under his fingers and the wind sifting through the brush, as if someone had slipped right through it.

He flicked open the paper. Black handwriting in big letters declared:

Payback is a bitch.

I've got someone you're looking for.

CHAPTER SIX

"Found her car," Carmen said, her voice tight over the phone.

Mark pressed the receiver to his ear, taking in the scene at the house. The chief's cruiser was pulling in, and Mark's dog had just come running back, though from where, he hadn't a clue.

"Where?" Mark asked, looking around, keenly aware that the feeling of being watched, which had prickled him moments ago, was now gone.

"Behind the crop of trees at the back of the house," she said. "If you walk past them, it opens to a big field of overgrown grass and brush. The driver's door is open. It was sitting right in the middle of the field, like someone got out and just walked away."

"On my way," Mark said, and hung up.

Carmen's cruiser was parked beside his Jeep. The chief was climbing out of his own car, wearing a ball cap and sunglasses, his badge pinned to a blue and white shirt, his gun holstered to his jeans. He stood beside his car, surveying the area, waiting for Mark to approach.

Mark opened the Jeep door and gestured for the dog to get in, running a hand over him, checking for injuries. "Stay here," he commanded. Between the note and Billy Jo's disappearance, he hadn't felt this kind of unease in a long time.

The chief was still looking around, saying nothing. Mark knew they would likely always butt heads, but he started toward him, lifting a hand in greeting.

"Carmen found Billy Jo's car," he said, gesturing with his thumb toward the back of the house.

The chief started walking, falling in beside him as Mark kept moving. "And what about this note on your Jeep? And the dog being gone? I see he's back."

Mark pulled the note out of his pocket, still sealed in the plastic bag he'd put it in. He held it out to the chief, wondering what he was thinking. The chief glanced at it, then handed it back.

"The dog just came back," Mark said. "I don't know what happened. If he could talk, it would be helpful. Maybe he followed whoever it was..."

The chief said nothing for a moment. "Take the dog back to the station. Gail will watch him and get that note off to the lab. Prints won't be quick, though. So, who'd you piss off, Mark? Because this is about you."

Mark was positive the chief preferred the dog over him, and the accusation stung. The blame game, as if he'd done something wrong. He fought the urge to roll his shoulders, fisting his hands as they kept walking. Carmen was visible in the distance, just past the trees, and he picked up his pace, digging into each step.

"If I knew who it was, you wouldn't be here," Mark said.

The chief walked beside him, easily keeping up, though he made a rude noise under his breath.

"Any idea who owns this place?" Mark asked. "I had

Carmen look into it, but when I found the note, she dropped everything to come here."

They continued along the trail, past trees and another overgrown field, until Billy Jo's green car came into view. Carmen lifted her hand, taking photos of the ground and the car.

"The Kenney family owned it until they sold it off years back," the chief said. "I think it's changed hands a few times, mostly to people from the mainland. The latest was someone with ideas about building a specialty alternative medical clinic for the super-rich, modeled after a private hospital in Switzerland. Permits were denied, though, and the island council shut it down. Last I heard, it was then sold to some multinational business or a foreigner from overseas. Your guess is as good as mine."

Mark wondered how the chief seemed to know all this, his ear to the ground, as if everything anyone did or had done crossed his desk. He said nothing as they walked. How had the car gotten all the way back here? He spotted tracks coming from another direction.

"Where does that trail lead?" he asked Carmen as he approached.

She was still taking photos with her phone—of the field, the tracks, and Billy Jo's car. Her dark hair was pulled back in a ponytail, her face, as always, free of makeup. She wore her standard brown deputy shirt.

"Over there?" He pointed to more trees when she didn't answer.

"It leads to the main road," she said. "It's unmarked. You'd have to know your way back here."

Mark watched as the chief leaned into the open car door and pulled out a big, bulky purse. He knew it was Billy Jo's. Just then, his cell phone rang, and Pam's name flashed on the screen.

"Hey," he answered, then cut Pam off before she could say anything. "I didn't see a text from you about which supervisor called Billy Jo." He turned his back on the chief and Carmen.

"I just got off the phone with Grant," Pam said. "He said no one is filling in for him. He doesn't know why someone would have called Billy Jo. When I told him I thought she said it was a Lane or a Lorne, he said there's no one there by that name, and he knows nothing about a call from last night. He said it had to be something else."

Mark had to bite back an F-bomb. Pam was doing something he didn't like. "You know what I want, Pam, is to talk to Grant. So while I appreciate you calling him, I asked you to send me his number. Billy Jo is missing, and we just found her car. She was at this address last night, so one of two things happened: someone from your agency called her and no one is communicating, which is a very real possibility, or whoever called her knows how you work. Regardless, I want to talk to Grant. Send me his number," he bit out. Even he could hear the sharpness in his tone, but he wasn't about to share anything with Pam about the note—how this seemed to be about him, how it was entirely his fault.

How, what, where, why? He didn't have a clue.

"You found her car...?" She took a sharp breath.

"Pam, text me Grant's number. You did tell him I want to talk to him?"

There was a second of silence. "I was trying to help. I'll send you his number. He was just going into a meeting, though."

He shook his head. "Pam, let me do the detective work. Send me his number. If anyone else has talked to Billy Jo, I want to talk to whoever it is." He hung up, pulling in a breath, staring at his phone and the ground, keeping his back to the chief and Carmen, who were talking behind him.

He took a minute to get his head on straight as he heard

the ding and saw the text from Pam: *will send you everything.*
Then he turned to see the chief emptying Billy Jo's bag on
the hood of the car. The chief glanced his way, expecting
Mark to fill him in on the call.

"That was Pam," he said. "I'm just waiting on Grant's
number. Need to find out who called her."

The chief only nodded, and Mark didn't add anything
else.

Carmen pulled Billy Jo's phone out from the car and held
it up. "Phone's dead."

Of course it was.

He walked over to the scattered contents of her bag and
picked up a small notebook. A pen was tucked in and
fastened. He opened it to a page scrawled with "Whitney
Chandler" and what he deciphered as "Lane Fuller." Underneath, she'd underlined:

Filling in for Grant, program director?

Emergency placement.

No other info!

The last line was double underlined.

He picked up on her frustration. Not just pressed, the pen
tip had dug into the page, nearly tearing the paper. The
letters were angry and dark, as if she'd known even then that
something about the call didn't sit right.

That was Billy Jo. Suspicious, irritated, paying attention
even when half asleep and pissed off at the world.

Good girl, he thought, taking a second as he re-read her
notes, a familiar worry tightening in his gut for the woman he
was closer to than anyone.

"It was Lane. Right here." He pressed his finger to the
name on the paper. "She writes everything down, old school.
Can't help herself, which is good for us. This here is the
address. So how the hell did whoever this is get her name, her

number? Carmen, can you find out who called her cell phone?"

His phone dinged. He pulled it from his pocket to see another text from Pam. "It's the number of Billy Jo's boss, Grant." He held up his phone and stepped back before dialing, watching the chief and Carmen look through Billy Jo's car again. He took another step away as he listened to the ring.

"Grant—"

"This is Detective Mark Friessen." He cut the man off.

"Right, I was just speaking with Pam," Grant said. "She said Billy Jo is missing..."

Mark shook his head, feeling off. He wanted full cooperation, worry, and effort from everyone.

"Well, now you're speaking with me," he said. "Yes, she's missing. She got a call last night from a man who said his name was Lane Fuller, a program supervisor, telling her to pick up a girl named Whitney Chandler. The address she was given is where we are, and we've found her car in a field. Pretty sure someone moved it. So what can you tell me about this call?"

Silence. Grant let out a rough sigh. "Okay, I just went through this with Pam..."

"And now you're going through it with me. Last I checked, Pam isn't a cop, and this is now an active investigation. So right now, I want you to tell me everything about how this works. Let's start with who she got a call—"

"I told Pam any calls would come from me. No one is filling in." Grant hadn't let Mark finish, and being cut off was something Mark didn't like.

He could feel the clock ticking. He'd been at her place at 11:20 last night; it was now 12:57. Something was very wrong.

"So you're saying no one called her last night?" Mark asked. He wished Grant was sitting across from him, so he could look him in the eye and really bring the hammer down.

"No. Look, I have a meeting. If a call comes in, I'm the one who calls her. As I told Pam, it's likely she didn't give you all the facts. Someone probably called her directly, and it didn't come through here."

Grant sounded like he was about to blow him off.

"You don't sound too worried about Billy Jo," Mark said.

Based on that damn note, this was about him. So why did it seem connected with DCFS? He wanted the number that had called Billy Jo's cell.

"Look, I don't know what this is about, but nothing came through this office. Of course I'm concerned, but as I said, I have a meeting."

"Your meeting can wait. Finding Billy Jo is my top priority. I'm looking at her notes now. One thing about that girl: she writes everything down. Lane Fuller, a program supervisor, called her about a Whitney Chandler at this address, sometime between one and two last night."

"It sounds like someone is messing around," Grant said. "I have no report about a Whitney Chandler. I don't know who that is, and there's no one filling in for me. I've never heard of a Lane Fuller. Look, Detective, I really have to go. I'm not sure what else to add. I'm at a loss. A prank, maybe? Maybe your information is wrong. Of course, I'm worried about Billy Jo. She has cases to handle. If there's been foul play, I want resources to find her."

This was exactly what Mark didn't want to hear. He was getting more questions than answers.

"All resources are on this," he said. "So you're saying no one from social services called her last night. Someone is impersonating you? That doesn't sit right with me."

"Well, it doesn't sit right with me, either. If you hear anything, Detective, call me." Grant hung up.

Mark pulled the phone away, staring at it. Why would someone go to such elaborate lengths to create a scenario designed to drag Billy Jo out in the middle of the night? It was looking more and more like something other than a girl in trouble.

When he turned around, Carmen was nodding at something the chief had said. Both were looking at him.

"Let's get this car hauled out of here," the chief called out.

Mark wanted to hang his head. "That was Billy Jo's boss. They don't know a Lane Fuller. Whoever called Billy Jo last night had access to troubling details about her job."

Carmen was already tossing Billy Jo's belongings from the hood of the car back into her bag. "I'll get her phone recharged, find out where the call came from," she said, holding up the phone.

Mark realized the ball was in his court.

"We have tracks, too, from the rain," Carmen added. "It's still muddy in spots, but if you really look, you can see them heading back to the road." She gestured.

The chief was already looking down at the print in the drying mud, pointing in the direction it led.

"I'm going to have a look around, follow the tracks," Mark said. "All of this is beginning to feel personal. This is about me. Someone was watching me, and wherever Billy Jo is, I don't know what kind of danger she's in. Whoever this is couldn't have gone far."

It was time to call her parents, he realized—the kind of call he dreaded making.

The chief looked off in the distance, deep in thought. "Sure, except first things first, Mark. I want you making a list of everyone who has it in for you. As you say, that note is personal. You know it, and I know it. Carmen, find out who owns this place, who's staying here, and everything about it. We start there. Then, just maybe, we can find this girl." He closed the car door and gestured back to Mark. "Come on. Let's go. You have work to do. Start figuring out that list, and I'll take a look around this place, follow these tracks. I'll call in a friend I know who does tracking."

What was it with the chief and his friends?

"I'm better use here, following the tracks," Mark said. He knew he was pushing it when the chief dragged his gaze back over to him, and the look he gave him should have been enough of a warning.

"You're too close to this, Mark. This is personal for you— and I'm the chief, in case you forgot. I want that list of who has it in for you."

"I'm a cop. You have any idea how many people would have it in for me? It comes with the job. It could be anyone." He dragged his gaze over to Carmen, who said nothing, and then back to the chief.

Except even as he said it, names flashed hard and fast. Dean Arlen, the meth dealer who had smiled through bloody teeth and told him he knew where cops slept. The brother of a woman Mark had dated for three bad weeks, who had waited outside a bar one night with a tire iron and a grudge. Ray McKinnon, the deputy he'd crossed when he'd refused to cover a dirty stop. The father of a kid Mark had arrested after a robbery gone sideways, a man who had looked at him in court with a promise in his eyes.

Faces. Voices. Threats tossed at him like loose change.

None of them felt right.

Or maybe that was the problem. Maybe one of them did, and he'd just been too arrogant to see it.

"Then think on it, because there's someone angry enough with you that, from what I can figure, he set a trap Billy Jo McCabe walked right into. He knows enough about you to go after who you care about. Evidently, that's Ms. McCabe."

Mark dragged his hand over his face, knowing he was right.

"Come on, you two," the chief ordered. "Let's get moving. The clock is now ticking, and every second we stand here is time Ms. McCabe doesn't have."

Carmen grabbed the bag and started walking. Mark fell in behind her. The chief stayed by the car, looking around. It was times like this that Mark wondered how good the chief was at his job.

CHAPTER SEVEN

MARK STARED AT HIS RINGING PHONE, SEEING THE
Lancasters' number. For a moment, he felt a flicker of hope
that Billy Jo had shown up, and he'd drive over and have a
talk with her.

"Has she shown up?" he asked, stepping out of his Jeep
and holding the door while the dog jumped out.

There was silence for a second. "No, she hasn't," Lesley
said. "I was calling to see if you had any word."

He wanted to bang his head. Holding his cell phone to his
ear, he walked back into the station. Gail was at her desk, and
the dog strode to his bed and lay down. Gail was staring at
him with that concerned motherly gaze. He only shook his
head and ran his hand over the back of his neck.

"No, I was hoping she'd turned up there and that was why
you were calling. If I hear something, I'll let you know." He
was about to hang up. He didn't have time for these kinds of
calls.

"Okay, now I'm officially worried," Lesley said. "Lorne
and I were talking, and I think her parents should be notified.

If it were us, we'd want to know. I know you said not to call..."

He wondered for a moment if she was asking permission. He walked to his desk and opened the drawer to drop in his keys. "You know what? Call them," he said. "I was about to myself, but I think you're right. Let them know we're looking for her. But again, unless you hear something about Billy Jo or remember something you didn't tell me, calling me to check in won't help when I'm working and searching for her."

Gail lifted her gaze to him, likely because of his sharp tone.

"I'm so sorry for bothering you," Lesley said. "I understand, but we are worried, and I just wanted to check in, mainly because Chase McCabe will want more details than we have. He'll likely want to call you, and he'll ask for your number..."

"Give it to him. I'll fill him in on what I can, but this is an active investigation from this point on. I can't share anything else." He rubbed the back of his neck again. This unsettled feeling was the kind of worry he hadn't wanted to feel. Worse, he hated being the reason Billy Jo had been targeted.

This was entirely his fault, and he didn't have a clue why.

"So what can I tell them?" Lesley said. "From the little I know of Chase McCabe, he's going to want answers."

He let the phone slide away from his mouth and stopped at his desk. "Lesley, don't tell him anything. Just give him my number, and I'll talk to him. Look, I have to go, but if something comes up, call me. If you don't hear from me, it's because..."

"I know. You're working on the case. Oh, and, Detective?"

He had to remind himself there were others worried about Billy Jo, not just him. "Yes, Lesley, what is it?"

"Please find that girl."

He found himself nodding again, an ache in his chest.

"That's what I'm doing, Lesley." He hung up and dropped the phone on his desk, not having a clue where to start.

Carmen strode in, carrying Billy Jo's bag and phone.

"Give me her phone," he said. "Let me charge it. You call her cell phone provider and get access to the call records."

Carmen dumped the cell phone from a plastic bag onto his desk. He pulled out his own charger and plugged it in. The screen stayed black. He pressed the side button once, then again, and for a second the low battery symbol flashed before disappearing.

"Come on," he muttered.

"It's charging," Carmen said.

"It's taking too damn long."

He knew she'd have been on her cell phone the moment she climbed into her car, the moment she pulled out of that isolated property—not the kind of place he'd want to walk alone at night.

But Billy Jo had.

"I put a call in on the way back," Carmen said. "They said forty-eight hours, but—"

"Bullshit! They're dragging their feet. It takes less than eight. Call them back. Tell them you're not some rookie who can be brushed off by a company spiel. A social worker is missing, and her last call is likely—"

"You think I'm new at this?" Carmen cut him off, her dark eyes flashing with temper as she dumped Billy Jo's purse on her desk. "They said forty-eight, and I said no, it won't. I'm not some damn rookie who just started and doesn't know how things work. I was very clear with my expectation for them to call back in an hour. I told them not to blow me off, because word gets out quickly about a major cell phone company hindering the search for a missing social worker. They do not want to be responsible for something tragic happening because they dragged their feet. Besides, once that's charged enough, see if you can get in and find the number yourself." She angled her head.

At her desk, Gail held a pen between both hands, resting on her elbows, watching them as if they were her entertainment or she was about to mediate. "You two, don't start getting at each other's throats. Work together. Carmen, if you have any trouble with that cell phone company, I'll make a call. Mark, as soon as that phone is charged, see if you can figure out her passcode. In the meantime, get working on that list of who has an axe to grind with you. Tolly called and filled me in. Mark, do you have that note for me? I'll have it rushed to the lab on the next ferry off-island." She held out her hand.

Mark pulled the note from his pocket, the familiar scrawl a stark reminder of how personal this was. "Let me get a photo of it first," he said, resting it on the desk. He snapped a picture through the plastic and walked the two steps to Gail. When he handed it to her, she stared at it, then lifted her gaze.

"You know, Mark, in this line of work, you will make enemies. There's no way around it. Tolly knows this. Coming up with a list and narrowing it down is the quickest way to find her. Sit down. Start with one name, then another..."

He knew she meant well.

Billy Jo's phone lit again, a faint white flash, then went black.

Mark stared at it. "Damn it."

The dog lifted his head from the bed and gave a low whine, as if the tension in the room had finally gotten to him too.

Mark looked over. "You and me both."

"And just so you both know," Gail continued, "that property was sold two years back to an offshore company. Ownership is anonymous due to strict secrecy laws in their jurisdiction. It's basically a way to park money in real estate and protect against lawsuits. No development plans have been filed. It's kind of a shell game, considering the same offshore company owns two other properties on the island and a number of other places in the country. There's no contact information."

Mark just stared at Gail as she opened a file and stapled papers together.

"Come on, you two," she said. "You're staring at me as if you have no idea how it works."

He realized he didn't, and he could tell by Carmen's expression that she didn't either. "I don't, so explain it," he said.

Gail closed the file and reached for another. "When you own real estate, you build equity in the property and want to protect that asset. So, you form an offshore company that you control. Ownership is anonymous because of how the laws are set up. Bearer shares can be used for even more privacy. Since the whole idea is good investments, this offshore company can negotiate a loan and provide services to the property—anything from contracting to landscaping, renovation, roofing, and my personal favorite, daycare."

Mark couldn't stand still. He walked back to his desk, checked Billy Jo's phone again, then looked to Carmen, who was already glancing at her own cell as if willing the provider to call back.

Nothing.

He turned back to Gail. "And that helps us how?"

"Because money leaves tracks, even when people think it doesn't," Gail said, not missing a beat. "A home improvement loan can be secured from the offshore company, and that loaned money takes equity in the real estate as security, with no usury laws. Then the offshore company can charge very high rates of interest to move more money offshore, and to protect its interest, the company can file a lien against the property."

Carmen's phone buzzed. She snatched it up, looked at the screen, and swore under her breath. "Not them."

Mark dragged his hand over the back of his neck.

Gail pointed the pen at both of them as if they were kids in her kitchen instead of cops in the middle of a missing-persons case. "A trust deed document is then filed at the county level, which allows the offshore company to take a first lien position on the property after the senior mortgage debt is satisfied. If the worst happens—for example, if you're sued, go bankrupt, or if the economy turns—you've just protected your assets."

It took Mark a second, as he stared at Gail, to wonder how she knew all this. "Why? That property is nothing..." he started.

"That property has an annual growth of ten to fifteen percent, Mark, and it's worth something. If I were you, I'd look into local contracts for work on it." She stood, stacked the files, and lifted them.

The dog whined again, louder this time. Mark looked over to see him standing now, ears angled forward, watching the door as if he expected someone to walk in with answers.

No one did.

"How do you know all this?" Mark asked. She was just the chief's wife, but he was starting to realize he didn't under-stand her at all.

"I used to be a commercial banker in another life. I helped people like that hide their money and make more. Now, the list, Mark. Get to work." She tilted her head.

His cell phone rang. He picked it up and saw the name Chase McCabe. He let out a heavy sigh, knowing this was about to get real. Her father wasn't the kind of man to sit on the sidelines and wait for Mark to find his daughter. No, he'd likely be on the next ferry, sitting in that office, shoving his nose into every aspect of the investigation.

Billy Jo's phone lit up again beside his hand. This time, the screen held a second longer before dimming—still not enough charge to open, not enough to give him the number, not enough to give him anything.

The ticking clock in his head seemed to get louder.

"Detective Friessen," he said, leaning back in his chair.

"This is Chase McCabe. My daughter is missing. What's going on? What are you doing about it, and who took her?"

So it began, his conversation with an angry father. And it was beginning to look as if Billy Jo had been taken because of him.

CHAPTER EIGHT

SHE DIDN'T WANT TO DRINK THE WATER OR EAT THE sandwich. She'd been forced to use the bucket because she'd had to pee so bad, and now sweat slicked her skin. The thing about tin boxes was they became hot boxes as the day heated up. She wanted fresh air. She wanted out.

The smell from the bucket in the corner, sour and sharp, mixed with rust and old metal. Her shirt clung to her back, damp under her arms, and every breath she pulled in seemed to scrape across her dry throat. She wiped her forearm over her mouth and tasted salt.

"Hey, open the door!" she yelled. "I know you're out there!" She pounded on what she knew was a cargo container, likely on a flatbed for shipping. She didn't have a clue how she'd gotten in there.

She was still pounding when she heard a clang. The door opened, light spilled in, and so did a fresh breeze she immediately welcomed.

"If you don't stop, I'm going to gag you and tie you up," he said, reaching for the pail. He tossed the contents behind him, and she heard a splash. When he set it back in the corner, she knew he would close that door, and then she wouldn't get out.

"Wait! It's really hot in here. And how did I get in here? I remember knocking on the door, it opening, and you had a gun in my face. Next, I woke up here... How?" She gestured toward him.

He stood, staring at her with dark eyes. He wore a faded blue striped T-shirt, tattoos covering his right arm. He lifted the bag and pulled out the bottled water she'd left inside it. He tossed it to her, and she caught the small plastic bottle.

"Drink the water. It will work the drug out of your system. It was propofol. Jabbed you in the arm. Didn't expect you to go down so hard. It's what they use to knock you out before surgery. So you don't remember?"

She just stared at the water.

"Don't look so worried," he said. "I didn't poison it. The seal's not broken."

She didn't pull her gaze from him at first, but when she did, she saw he was right. The seal was intact. "I'd prefer it if you'd just let me go. I'll get my own water at home."

He didn't smile and didn't look away. Something in his gaze made her twist off the cap and take a swallow of the warm water, gross but wet.

The water hit her stomach too fast, and for a second she thought she might bring it back up. She forced herself to stop, to breathe through her nose, to save some even though every part of her wanted to drain the bottle dry. She had no idea when he'd open that door again.

"The sandwich is from the coffeehouse," he said. "Again, I haven't drugged it. Eat something or don't, but I'm not letting you out."

She took in the half-opened door, knowing the other side would be locked. He stood there as she took in what she was positive had to be an old barn or shed behind him, sunlight streaming in from cracks in the old wood. What time was it? Early afternoon.

Why couldn't she remember being stuck with a needle? Maybe it was the shock of having a gun in her face, but all she could recall was the cold steel, wondering if that would be her last breath. "So this is about Mark? Well, I hate to tell you, but the detective and I only know each other from working together. We're not close."

The man didn't pull his gaze.

She lifted her water, wondering how that lie had rolled so easily off her tongue.

"There's something about small towns," he said. "They like to talk, and an island like this is no exception. You're really not in a position to lie." He gestured around them.

"Then you would know that Mark and I help each other out with cases and all, but that's it," she said. "I'm not exactly his type. Last I knew, he was involved with..."

"The attractive, leggy blonde who runs the coffeehouse?" the man said. "He's a guy. Mark's always gone for the wrong kind. Now he's avoiding her, and she's avoiding him, and everyone in town knows it. Love gone wrong. Seems to be a knack Mark has."

The way he said it made her pause. She lifted the bottle of water to her lips, realizing he knew Mark well—too well. Who the hell was this guy?

"So, what, is that an excuse for men's superficial taste?" she said.

He made a face, twisting his lips in humor or disgust. "Guys like hot women, but that doesn't mean they want to settle with them. Mark evidently hasn't figured that out yet. Shouldn't sell yourself short, because people see the way he looks at you."

Okay, that was not what she wanted to hear, because it brought back the image of him from her dream, the way he'd looked at her. She was still angry over something she'd never share with anyone.

"Well, the problem with a small town, an island community, is that talk is just that: talk. People see us, and we work well together, so they figure there has to be something more. So what is your name?" She took a swallow of water before screwing the top back on, saving half. She didn't want to use the bucket again.

"You think I don't know what you're doing? Trying to find out who I am isn't important." His hand was on the door, about to close it. "You think you're smarter than me, too..."

"Wait, seriously, just stay and talk for a bit," she pleaded. "I need the breeze, the air. If you don't want to tell me your name, fine, but I'm just saying it would be nice to have an idea what to call you."

Was he from the island? She didn't think so. She'd never seen him before, but then, she knew she hadn't met everyone in Roche Harbor.

He said nothing, likely thinking. If she didn't keep him talking, that door would close, and quickly.

"I guess I'm at a loss as to what you have against Mark," she ventured. "He did something to you?"

This was personal. She knew so much about Mark and the things that haunted him, but there were always things you never truly knew about someone.

The man had a tic, twitching his lips when he was considering something or she was pissing him off.

"Look, I don't know what this is or why you're so angry," she continued, her voice firm. "You said there was no Whitney, but you know who I am. I'm a social worker here. I help kids. I don't hurt people. It wasn't you who phoned me. I know voices. So who called me?"

He only shook his head. "Not me who called, but you already know that. I made a call. I knew who to call to have you knocking on the door. Again, you keep asking questions as if you think I'm going to open up and talk to you, share everything. I told you I have business with Mark, unfinished business, and you're the means to it..."

"You didn't call me," she repeated, a challenge in her tone.

His gaze shifted, just once, toward the door.

There.

It was quick, so quick she could have missed it if she hadn't spent her life watching people for the things they didn't say. Someone else had helped him, or he wanted her to think someone had. Either way, this wasn't just some angry man with a gun and a cargo container. There was more here, something with moving parts she couldn't see.

"So who did?" she pressed. "Because whoever it was knew enough about DCFS to get me out here."

His hand tightened on the edge of the door. "You said there used to be a Whitney Chandler. Is this about her? Did something happen?"

He made a face that revealed teeth missing on one side. "You like bedtime stories, Billy Jo?" The way he said it, she knew she should say no.

"Not particularly, but then, I didn't grow up with parents who told bedtime stories. Tell me anyway."

He only nodded. She realized he didn't know everything about her. Good.

"Imagine living in a place, being part of a family where your sister had to hitchhike because no one could afford a car," he started. "There's the insurance and the license, but then, even driving schools and places to get your license aren't accessible to everyone because they won't accept certain IDs. Because of where your family lives, finding work is hard, and your sister has to look further and further away. She gets a job at a truck stop restaurant, but the job is twenty miles away, and she needs to hitch rides or walk to get there.

"One day, she's just not there. Breakfast is ready. She should have been home in bed, sleeping, but her bed was never slept in. Imagine your mother going into her room and seeing her bed is still made, then realizing she didn't come home. Did she stay over at a friend's and forget to call? So your mother starts calling neighbors, friends. 'Have you seen her?' But no one has.

"When the police were finally called, as the sun went down, all they knew was that your sister had vanished. Of course, they assumed she ran away. Who wouldn't want to escape this life? They assumed she did drugs, drank, got herself into trouble. There had to be trouble at home, or she was looking for trouble, selling herself, because that's what girls like her do, according to the cops. Walking along a highway, hitching a ride—suddenly, that creates the assumption she was asking for it."

The air shifted, the breeze cutting off as his body blocked the opening. Heat settled back over her shoulders. Billy Jo rolled the water bottle between her hands, hearing the thin plastic crackle. Her mouth was dry again, and she hated that he had that too—her water, her air, the door.

She had a feeling she knew where this was going. "She went missing," she said. "Was this Whitney?"

His hand was still on the door. She could see he was being dragged into a memory, but the way he stood there, big and angry, there was no affection for her. "You know, cell phone companies don't provide service in areas where Whitney is from. They provide it where they can make money, and most communities like hers don't have reliable coverage. There's an entire stretch of highway that's dark, with no service. When you're having to hitch a ride because there's no bus, with no way to call for help..."

Where was she from? He still hadn't said who she was.

"She disappeared. Who was she to you? A family member? A friend?"

He lifted his gaze. In his dark eyes, where she had expected to see sadness, there was only anger. "I was sixteen, and she was seventeen—my sister. I told her to be careful, said I would go with her if she had to hitch, but I didn't that one time. The kind of guys who drive that highway...you don't want your sister alone with them. They're transient workers who man the camps, from oil pipelines to mining."

A faint scrape or thump came from somewhere outside the container, beyond the barn wall. Billy Jo stilled, listening, but the man didn't turn around. Maybe it was just the building shifting in the heat. Maybe a bird. Maybe someone else.

Her fingers tightened around the bottle.

She pulled in a breath and leaned against the metal wall. It was hot through her shirt, and she shifted away, wishing he'd just say everything. "I know it's a problem, and no one with power wants to do anything about it. I know those camps breed everything bad—drugs, alcohol, violence..." Then there were the girls. The sex trade, the social workers had called it—girls as young as fourteen, and what those men did to them, voluntary or not. "But I know it's about the bigger picture. A camp is needed for these workers to build their pipelines, to work the oilfields, to mine the area. The oil and mining companies that own them can't be touched. It's angered many. Is that what happened to her?" She hoped not, but she feared where he was going.

"Living on the res, there are so many strikes against you to begin with," he said. "Poverty, poisoned water, no hope. Those camps are too close to Indian reservations, some built right on them, because the land is owned by the Feds. If a big company wants it, they get it. Native women are hunted, assaulted. They go missing in and around these camps, never to be found again. Why is it so easy? When you live and breathe that life on the res, it feels like an evolution from the residential schools to this—continually being raped, over and over.

"You understand, growing up, that you're nothing. Your sisters, your mothers, their daughters are hunted by men because whatever a man does to a woman on the res, he cannot be arrested or prosecuted by tribal authorities. And because it's res land, the county sheriff has no jurisdiction. Again, these oil workers walk free. They know this, and yet no one does anything about them. These guys know you can't assault or kill her outside the reservation, but you can do anything to her on the res and nothing will happen to you."

A bead of sweat ran between her shoulder blades. She reached up and wiped under her chin with the back of her hand, then took another careful swallow of water, hating how loud it sounded in the metal box. The bucket was back in the corner, empty now but still stinking, and the sandwich sat untouched in the bag. Her stomach turned at the smell, at the heat, at the story he was laying out as if it had been carved into him, one sentence at a time.

She really looked at him then. She realized now that he wasn't white. He was Native, after vengeance. She knew all too well that decades of murdered and missing Indigenous women would never find justice. But how the hell did Mark fit into this?

"Is that what happened to Whitney? Was she killed, assaulted? Is this about justice for her?"

Emotion flickered across his face. This story had no happy ending. "She didn't come home from work. She was seventeen. These transient oil workers move from state to state, camp to camp, often on or near tribal lands where these camps are built. I knew what had happened; twenty-five women had gone missing in five years. Every camp that goes up brings more crime, more missing women—Indigenous women, prostitutes, no one who matters. No one looks, and the workers move on. Whitney was my sister." His hand rested on the door.

"And what does Mark have to do with this? I know him. He wouldn't look the other way."

There it was, the anger again, the moment she knew he was going to shut down. "The tribal police were called, but they have next to no resources. So the sheriff from the next county was called in. And who did they send? A wet-behind-the-ears Mark Friessen. He showed up with a badge, a gun, and nineteen days on the job. The sheriff couldn't and wouldn't interrupt her dinner to drive out or even pretend Whitney mattered. We called everyone, pushed and pushed, but her body hadn't been found yet. Then her purse and phone were discovered in one of the camps.

"An oil worker, a man in his forties, was arrested, but he walked out of the sheriff's office before the ink was cold. Her body was found on the res shortly after. An anonymous tip came in while the guy was being driven to the station. They couldn't prosecute because of where she'd been found. Oil company executives were waiting to pick him up, and he was moved to another state, another camp. No one knew where. It's easy to disappear. Mark Friessen showed up, hat in hand, along with that prick of a sheriff, saying there was nothing they could do. The law was the law, and it was now a federal issue. The Feds have declined to do anything."

There would have been so many strikes against Whitney, she knew.

A fly buzzed near the bucket, hitting the wall once, then again. Billy Jo watched it for a second, watched it throw itself at the same hot metal as if there had to be a way through if it just kept trying.

"I'm not surprised, and it's not right," Billy Jo said. "You have every right to be angry. I know the Feds have jurisdiction, and I know they've refused to investigate and prosecute more than two-thirds of all the cases. Those camps are a safe haven for sexual predators. But I don't understand what Mark did. You're angry at him for not being able to do his job, for having his hands tied? I know Mark well..."

"Oh, I know you do. I made a point of learning everything I could about the tribal police—who were useless—about the county sheriff—who couldn't even remember my sister's name—and about the oil worker. The one who walked out of the sheriff's office, climbed into a fancy SUV with the oil company name on the plate, and was taken back to the camp where my sister's belongings were found. But he was gone the next day, off to another state, another camp. You know what Mark Friessen said to me when I showed up in the sheriff's office, demanding a name, demanding they do something for my sister?"

His voice was low, and she picked up on a bitterness that suggested he wasn't about to be reasoned with. "He told me to walk out that door and look after my mother, my family, to get a job and a car. He pointed out that if my sister hadn't hitchhiked, she'd likely still be alive. That was after I heard the sheriff tell him to find out what I wanted and get me out of his office."

She just stared for a moment, stunned. Had Mark really said that? She'd have given anything to be face to face with him right now and ask him what the hell he'd been thinking.

The air in the container seemed thinner. She pulled in a breath and felt it catch, not from the heat this time, but from the image of Mark saying those words. A younger Mark with a badge and a gun and all that arrogance, before life had stripped enough from him to leave scars.

"So you've been watching Mark, following him?" she said.

"For what, payback? I don't understand. Why not go after the oil worker who killed your sister?"

His lips pulled into something that gave her a sick feeling in her stomach and tightened the knot that had settled there even more.

"Who says I didn't?" he said. He reached for the bag and tossed it to her. "Eat your sandwich and get comfortable, because you could be here for a while. If you keep the ruckus up, as I said, I will gag you and tie you up."

Then, before she could say another word, he slammed the door. The clang of the bar locking her in echoed in the sudden silence.

Darkness closed around her again, thick and hot.

Billy Jo stood there, the bag in one hand, the half-empty bottle in the other, listening. His boots moved away across the floor outside. Then nothing.

No engine. No voices.

Just the heat, the stink of the bucket, and the awful knowledge that someone else had made the call that brought her here.

———————————————

CHAPTER NINE

———————————————

MARK TRIED TO FIGURE OUT BILLY JO'S PASSCODE, knowing her dad was already on his way to the island, having demanded every detail Mark couldn't share. How long until Chase walked through the door and likely made his life a living hell? He'd heard it in Chase's voice: The man wasn't going to wait for anyone to call him or swallow any part of his official response.

"I can't talk about an ongoing investigation," Mark had said.

"Don't give me that bureaucratic bullshit," Chase had replied. "I'm one call away from going over your head."

Of course, Mark believed him.

"I'm looking," Mark said. "We don't know why she was taken. Someone called her, and we're waiting on the number from the cell phone company. Her car was found in an abandoned field, her cell phone was dead, and her purse was there too. But we have no idea who called her because DCFS has no report about a girl in trouble or a program supervisor named Lane Fuller."

Mark neglected to offer up the note or the fact that this

was likely because of him. Maybe that was why he felt so damn guilty now as he typed in her birthdate, her age, her address, and her license number into her phone, but came up with nothing.

"You still can't get into her phone?" Carmen called out from her desk.

He could hear Gail on the phone, talking—to whom, he didn't know. The chief still hadn't come back, and the computer screen in front of him displayed a list of names, from the deputies he'd worked with, to everyone he'd arrested, to every girl he'd dated. He had to pull his hand over his face, unsettled.

"No," he said. "I can't figure out her passcode. Her birthdate, driver's license number, address..."

"Try one two three four," Carmen said.

He stared at her. "You're serious? There's no way..." But he typed it in, and it unlocked. "How did you know?" He sat up, opening her recent calls.

"It's what so many people do," was all she said.

He would have to remember that, considering he used the same numbers his brother Danny did—a sequence of his mom's, dad's, and brother's month and day of birth. He'd thought he'd been creative.

"Okay, here it is. The call came in at one eighteen a.m. The number is..." He rattled it off.

Carmen typed the number into her computer, then frowned, shooting him an odd expression. "The number is from another cell phone provider, but it's registered to DCFS on the mainland."

He hadn't expected that. He rose from his chair and moved to her computer as she slid the screen around for him to see.

"See? It's right there. Doesn't say the name, but the cell phone company would already be pulling that."

"Lane Fuller, from DCFS in Olympia," Gail said, hanging up the phone and holding a piece of paper. "The cell phone company just called back. Isn't that the name you wrote down, Mark? The call was from Lane Fuller at DCFS, the county's head office."

He looked at Carmen, who leaned back in her chair. "Didn't you talk to her boss, Grant? And he said..."

"He said he didn't know a Lane Fuller," Mark cut in, a muscle ticking in his jaw. "That lying piece of shit..." He wondered if Grant made a habit of lying to the police. "Grant said no one was filling in for him, and he had no record of a missing girl named Whitney Chandler." Mark walked back to his desk, each step heavy, feeling like he was being strung along. He reached for his cell phone and dialed Grant's number. "Dammit! I hate being lied to."

He listened to the ring, feeling both women's eyes on him, more confused than ever about who Lane Fuller was.

It went straight to voicemail: "You've reached the personal mailbox of Grant Webber. I can't take your call. Leave a message, and I'll call you right back. If this is an emergency, dial zero and speak to the operator."

He heard the beep and drew in a breath. "Grant, this is Detective Friessen. I need you to call me back." He pressed end, avoiding Gail's and Carmen's gazes, though he could feel them watching him.

Had Grant realized his screwup and was now hiding like a coward? Mark grabbed Billy Jo's phone, pulled up that number again, and dialed. It rang once, twice...

"Lane Fuller."

His stomach lurched. He stared at Carmen, who was now standing.

"Did you just say Lane Fuller, with DCFS?" Mark asked, his voice tight.

"Yes, and who is this?"

He fought the urge to roll his shoulders, glancing at the clock, seeing the wasted time tick by. "Detective Mark Friessen, from Roche Harbor. You called Billy Jo McCabe last night about a girl in trouble...?" He snapped his fingers at Carmen, wanting the notebook with the girl's name. She pulled it from Billy Jo's bag and handed it to him.

"Roche... Harbor?" Lane said, a pause suggesting he was trying to place it on a map. "Sorry, Detective, which county is that again?"

Mark stared at the phone.

Carmen's gaze narrowed; she'd heard it too.

"You called one of our social workers in the middle of the night and sent her out here," Mark said, his voice level only because Gail was now watching him. "You don't know where Roche Harbor is?"

"I handle calls from several regions," Lane said. "It was an emergency placement that came through after hours. I don't normally—"

"Billy Jo McCabe," Mark cut in. "You called her."

There was a pause, then the faint click of keys. "Uh, yes, I did. McCabe, you said? What is this about?"

For a second, Mark could only listen to the man breathe. He'd sent Billy Jo out into the dark, to a rural address, for a child no one could seem to find in the system, and the man had to ask her last name again.

Mark's hand tightened around the phone, knuckles aching.

He shook his head. Gail had picked up the phone; he'd thought she had the chief on the line. Mark opened the notebook to the page where Billy Jo had scribbled the names.

"This is about the fact that Billy Jo is now missing, and no one knows anything about a girl named Whitney Chandler."

Silence stretched on the other end. "I don't understand

what you're talking about. Who did you say you are again, a detective?"

"That's right, Detective Mark Friessen, Roche Harbor Police Department. We were called this morning by Pam Hunt, who runs the local DCFS office. Billy Jo didn't show up with the girl she was supposed to pick up and take to an emergency placement. What I don't understand is that I spoke with Grant Webber this morning, and there seems to be a big question mark about who you are. Worse, no one knows anything about a girl named Whitney Chandler."

"Hang on a second." Lane's voice was rough. Mark heard him breathing, typing into a computer. Mark fisted his hand, wanting to swear at the man to hurry the fuck up. "Unfortunately, this sometimes happens. Her name isn't in the system, but yes, a call came in late and was passed to me since I was on call last night. I was to give it to the local office. I see the paperwork isn't in the system. It doesn't always get filed and input. It's likely sitting on the service desk. But yes, I remember the call. You say she didn't pick up the child?"

He knew he was shaking his head, fighting the urge to yell through the phone. He wanted to sit down with Grant to ask him what the fuck he was doing. "No, she did not. In fact, Billy Jo appears to be missing. We have the address you gave her..." He glanced at her notes and read it off.

Behind him, the station door opened, and the chief walked in. Mark glanced back at the notebook. Carmen was now with the chief, and he couldn't make out what they were talking about.

Something rustled in the background. "That's the address I have. You say she's missing. Maybe she's at home...?"

"Look, missing means not at home, not at work. We found her car abandoned in a field. Where did the call about this Whitney Chandler come from?"

Papers rustled in the background, and Mark gritted his teeth, suspecting what Lane would say next.

"You know what?" Lane said. "I'm going to have to get back to you on that."

That was exactly what Mark hadn't wanted to hear. He wanted to bang his head against the wall. "Well, you do that. And while you're at it, why do Billy Jo's notes say you're a program supervisor filling in for Grant, her boss? When I spoke with Grant, he had no idea who you were. Do you not communicate over there?" He gestured widely, aware of how sharp the accusation sounded as everyone in the room watched him.

The man cleared his throat. "I am a program supervisor, but I don't know Grant. Haven't met him. I'm just one of many, so it's an easy mistake. I don't normally take calls for that area, but sometimes it's the luck of the draw. Let me get back to you."

Luck of the draw.

Mark closed his eyes for a half second. Billy Jo wasn't a draw. She wasn't a name on a form tossed from one desk to another. She was out there somewhere because this man had treated a call like a box to check before moving on to the next one.

He knew the man would likely hang up and never call back. "That would be great. I appreciate it. Do you want my number so you can call me back?"

The man hesitated, then cleared his throat. "I guess that would be helpful."

Mark would have given anything to see his face as he called him out on this screwup. He rattled off his cell phone number. "So when can I expect a call from you? Considering one of your social workers is missing."

Lane cleared his throat again. "I'll find out right now from the call center where the call came from and call you right back." Then he hung up.

Mark lowered his phone, wondering how deeply flawed a system was that was supposed to be doing what was best for kids.

"Well...?" the chief said.

Mark dropped his cell phone on the desk. "Seems there is a Lane Fuller, and he did call Billy Jo last night, but he doesn't know offhand where the call came from. Evidently, he's looking into it now. So at least we know it really was a DCFS person who called her last night. The question is, whoever left the note on my Jeep—is he the same person who called DCFS?"

The chief only nodded, then glanced at Gail. "Well, while we wait, you have that list of names?"

Mark turned the screen for the chief to see. "Where do you want to start? The ex-girlfriends, the felons I put away, or the cops who hate me?"

All eyes were on his list.

Carmen looked from the screen to Mark, then to the chief. "Didn't you say, Chief, that one of the neighbors mentioned a contractor working on the property? A caretaker?"

The chief shrugged. "Could be. He wasn't sure. Only spotted him once or twice. Mel Brooks, at the end of the road, thinks he might have a card or something. He's looking for it and will call me back."

Gail handed a file to the chief. "That's fine, but while you all wait with your thumbs up your asses for a call back, there's this thing called cell phones. You can work while you wait. These are the addresses of two other properties on the island owned by the same company that owns the property where Billy Jo called from. So, Mark, how about you take the one at the south end, and Carmen, you take the north?"

There it was, Gail giving marching orders.

Mark reached for the paper, scanning the address, then glanced at the dog. "Come on, boy," he called, and the dog rose, following him to the door. He stepped out, Carmen behind him. As she pulled the door closed, the dog trotted to the Jeep and lifted his leg on the back tire.

"Wait up!" Carmen said, hurrying after him.

He turned to her, noting how she always seemed to hold her cards close.

"The chief said something else when you were on the phone," she said. As she looked away, the unease in his stomach sharpened.

"And that was?" He lifted his gaze back to the station. Through the glass door, he could see the chief and his wife in conversation.

"He said after he walked the property, he found a second set of tracks—tire tracks—over by the road, where the car was driven in. And there's something else. One of the neighbors down the road thought he saw a truck parked just off the road before lunch."

He stared at her, the implication sinking in. "The same time I was there."

She nodded.

"Likely who put the note on my Jeep."

She nodded again.

He lifted his gaze to the station window. Why did it feel as if, at every step of this investigation, someone was holding something back? "Thanks, Carmen. Call me from that other property. Let me know what you find."

She strode to her police cruiser, and Mark opened the door for the dog, who climbed in. That unsettled feeling returned. Secrets and lies...

Someone was playing with him. He just hoped he could

figure this out and find Billy Jo before her dad showed up and discovered his daughter was caught up in something because of him.

CHAPTER TEN

MARK HAD ONE HAND ON THE JEEP DOOR WHEN THE station's front door opened behind him.

"Detective!"

He turned, expecting Gail, maybe the chief changing his mind, or Carmen with one more thing she hadn't said inside. The dog was already in the passenger seat, panting through the open window, watching him with dark, trusting eyes, as if he had any idea where they were going.

Carmen was halfway to her cruiser, the paper Gail had given them folded in her hand. Two addresses. One north. One south. Two properties owned by the same offshore company as the place where Billy Jo's car had been found. It wasn't much, but it was more than sitting around with their thumbs up their asses, as Gail had so politely put it.

Mark was about to ask Carmen what now when a man came around the side of the building fast, a woman beside him.

He knew who it was before the man said a word.

Chase McCabe looked exactly like the kind of father who

would take a float plane rather than wait for a ferry. Tall, broad-shouldered, his face hard, pale around the mouth, his eyes sweeping once over the lot, over the Jeep, over Carmen, before landing on Mark.

Rose McCabe was beside him, blond hair windblown, one hand wrapped around her purse strap. She looked past Mark to the station, then to the Jeep, then to the dog, searching.

Looking for Billy Jo.

For one awful second, Mark saw the hope in her eyes, that instinctive mother's search, as if her daughter might be somewhere just out of sight, coming around the building, walking out the station door, mad as hell and ready to tell everyone to stop fussing.

Then Rose didn't see her.

Something in her face changed.

Mark stepped away from the Jeep.

"Where is my daughter?" Chase said.

No greeting. No handshake. No wasted breath.

Mark pulled in a slow breath. There was no good answer. "We're looking for her."

Chase came closer. "That's what you said on the phone. It wasn't enough then, and it sure as hell isn't enough now."

The station door opened again, and Gail stepped out first, her gaze moving from Chase to Rose and then to Mark. Behind her came the chief, big and unreadable, his ball cap tugged low, his eyes already taking in the scene.

"Mr. McCabe, Mrs. McCabe," Tolly said. "I'm Chief Shepard. Why don't you come inside and we'll—"

"No," Chase said.

The word was quiet, but it stopped everyone.

Carmen had come back over now, standing off to Mark's left. She said nothing, but he could feel her watching, feel her taking in every word.

Chase didn't pull his gaze from Mark. "I talked to you on the phone. You said her car was found. You said she was missing. You didn't say enough. So I'm asking again. Where is my daughter?"

Mark felt heat crawl up the back of his neck. "We don't know yet."

Rose made a small sound, swallowing it before it could become something else. Mark looked at her then—a mistake. She looked too much like every parent he'd ever faced with no answers. Only this time, it was Billy Jo.

Billy Jo, who would hate this.

Billy Jo, who would tell them all to stop looking at her like she was already dead.

Billy Jo, who had been taken because someone wanted *him*.

Chase's gaze sharpened. He saw it. Of course he did. He was a lawyer, a father, and from everything Billy Jo had never said but somehow carried, not a man who missed much.

"What aren't you saying?" Chase asked.

"Chase," Rose said, her voice thin.

Mark looked at the chief.

Tolly's expression didn't change, but his eyes did. Warning. *Careful.*

Mark didn't have the patience for careful.

"Someone left a note," he said.

Gail's gaze snapped to him. Carmen went still.

Chase didn't move. "What note?"

Mark reached inside his jacket, then remembered Gail had the original, already bagged for the lab. He pulled his phone from his pocket instead, opened the photo he'd taken, and held it out.

Chase took the phone.

Rose stepped closer, then stopped as if the words on the

screen had reached out and slapped her. Her hand went to her mouth, but she didn't cry. Mark had a feeling Billy Jo had learned that from her too—that rigid way of taking a hit and not letting anyone see how bad it hurt.

Chase read the words once. Then again.

Payback is a bitch.

I've got someone you're looking for.

Then he looked up slowly.

"This is about you," he said.

Mark didn't look away. "Yes."

"And my daughter is missing because of you."

The words landed hard, exactly where Mark already knew they belonged.

"Chase," Rose said again.

Mark nodded once. "That's how it looks."

The chief stepped forward. "We don't know that yet."

Chase turned his head. "Then you'd better start knowing something."

Tolly's jaw worked once. "We are doing everything we can."

"Are you?" Chase said. "Because from where I'm standing, my daughter was sent into the dark by someone pretending there was a child in trouble. Her car was found abandoned. Her phone was dead. Her bag was left behind. And now I'm looking at a note that says someone has her because of him." He jabbed a finger toward Mark. "So don't hand me procedure, Chief. Don't hand me the official line. I've heard it before from men in better suits than yours."

The parking lot went quiet.

Somewhere behind them, gulls cried over the harbor. A truck rolled past, tires humming over wet pavement. Inside the Jeep, the dog whined, low and uneasy, as if he knew exactly what kind of storm had just walked into Mark's day.

Rose moved past Chase and stopped beside the Jeep. She didn't touch the dog, only looked through the open window at the seat, at the police radio, at the empty place where Billy Jo should have been if this day had been different.

"She had her phone with her?" Rose asked.

Mark swallowed. "It was in her car. Battery was dead."

Rose nodded, her gaze still fixed on the Jeep. "She never remembers to charge the damn thing."

The words came out with such raw, ordinary frustration that Mark had to look away.

Then Rose looked back at him. "Was she scared?"

He had no answer for that.

He could picture Billy Jo in the rain, pulling up to that house, angry at herself, probably muttering under her breath, telling herself to get it together. He could picture her knocking on that door because some girl named Whitney Chandler needed help. He could picture the door opening.

His throat tightened. "I don't know."

Rose's eyes filled, but she blinked back the tears. "She would have been mad first."

That nearly broke something in him.

"Yeah," he said. "She would have."

The station phone rang inside, sharp enough that Gail turned her head.

For one second, no one moved.

Then Gail went back in, heels tapping fast across the floor. Through the glass, Mark saw her pick up. She listened, then looked through the door at him and lifted her hand.

"Mark," she called out. "Lane Fuller. Says he found where the complaint came from."

Mark was already moving.

He stepped inside, Chase right behind him, Rose following, the chief and Carmen coming in after. The dog barked once from the Jeep, and Mark pointed at him through the window. "Stay."

Of course, the dog only stared back.

Inside, Gail had the line on hold, her hand over the receiver. Billy Jo's phone was still on Mark's desk, plugged in and dark, her notebook open beside it. The list of names was on his computer screen: men he'd arrested, men he'd embarrassed, men who had threatened him in courtrooms, on roadsides, through the bars of holding cells. Ex-girlfriends. One angry brother of an ex-girlfriend. A former deputy who'd told him he was a self-righteous son of a bitch and would get his someday.

Too many names.

None of them felt right.

This was too patient. Too personal. Too damn careful.

Gail put the call through. "Line one."

Mark grabbed the receiver. "Talk."

There was a pause on the other end, a rustle of paper, then Lane Fuller cleared his throat. "Detective Friessen, I pulled what I could from intake. The call came through the emergency line just after midnight. Anonymous male caller. The report was incomplete, but he gave the child's name as Whitney Chandler and said there was an immediate risk if we didn't send someone."

Mark tightened his grip on the phone. "Where did the call originate?"

"We're still trying to determine that. It appears the caller blocked the number, or it was routed through—"

"That's not an answer."

Another pause. "No, it isn't."

Mark heard the slow, deliberate typing. Too damn slow.

"Read me the intake note," Mark said.

"I'm not sure I can—"

"Read it."

Gail had gone still. Carmen was already at her computer, fingers flying across the keyboard. Chase stood close enough now that Mark could feel him listening.

Lane exhaled. "Caller reports minor female, Whitney Chandler, in immediate danger at rural residence. Caller states local DCFS should send Billy Jo McCabe, as she handles difficult girls and has prior experience with emergency placements."

Mark went cold.

The receiver creaked in his hand.

"He asked for Billy Jo by name?" he said.

Chase stepped closer.

"That's what the note says," Lane replied. "I didn't see that part last night. I was on call, and the report came through as urgent. I contacted the local worker listed for emergency placements."

"You didn't see it," Mark said.

"Detective, it was after one in the morning. Intake was short-staffed, the information was coming in fast, and I—"

"No. You didn't see it. You didn't verify it. You didn't call her supervisor. You didn't call law enforcement. You sent her out there alone."

No one in the room said a word.

Lane cleared his throat again, and Mark wanted to reach through the phone and drag him across the desk. "The caller stated police involvement would escalate the situation and place the child at greater risk."

Mark shut his eyes for one second.

Because of course he had.

Whoever had done this knew the language. Knew the pressure points. Knew how to make a social worker move fast and alone. Knew enough about Billy Jo to know she wouldn't wait when a child was in trouble.

"And you bought that?" Mark said.

"I followed protocol based on the information provided."

Mark laughed once, a sound devoid of amusement. "Your protocol just walked a woman into a trap."

Lane didn't answer.

Mark opened his eyes. "I want the recording of that call."

"There may be a process—"

"You start that process now. You preserve the recording, the intake notes, the routing data, every timestamp, every person who touched that call. If one piece of that disappears, I will personally drive to Olympia and make your life a living hell. Do we understand each other?"

Lane's voice changed. "Yes."

"And Fuller?"

"Yes?"

"If you remember anything else, if you find anything else, if someone in that office so much as sneezes near this report, you call me. Not Grant. Not Pam. Me."

"I understand."

Mark hung up before the man could say anything more, his hand lingering on the receiver.

He looked down at the list on his desk. So many names. Men who hated him. Men who could have left that note.

But this wasn't only about him.

Whoever had Billy Jo knew her too.

Her job. Her habits. Her willingness to show up. Her damn need to save every kid because no one had saved her until Chase McCabe found her with a gun in her hand and rage in her bones.

Mark dragged both hands over his face.

Chase's voice was low beside him. "He knew her name."

Mark nodded. "Yes."

"He knew what would get her out of bed."

"Yes."

Rose pressed a hand to her chest, looking away.

Carmen stood. "I'm going to pull everything I can on Whitney Chandler."

Mark looked over to her. "Do it. Missing persons, old county reports, anything connected to that name. Have Gail keep digging when we leave."

"Already on it," Carmen said, of course.

The chief stepped closer. "Mark."

He turned.

Tolly's gaze was hard, but something else was there now. Not sympathy—Mark didn't want sympathy. Maybe it was calculation. Maybe it was recognition that this was worse than they'd thought.

"Sit down," the chief said. "Think. Who would know both of you well enough to set this up?"

Mark let out a breath. "Everyone on this island talks."

"Not everyone knows DCFS procedure," Carmen said.

Gail tapped the paper she'd already handed them. "And not everyone has access to empty rural properties where a woman could disappear without being seen."

Mark looked down at the two addresses again.

One north. One south.

The same two leads they'd been about to check before Chase and Rose arrived and Lane Fuller called back with one more reason for Mark to want to put his fist through a wall.

He reached for his keys again.

"Where are you going?" Chase said.

"To check the only leads we have."

Chase moved with him. "I'm coming."

"No," Mark said.

Chase's expression hardened.

Mark stepped close, lowering his voice. "You come with me, you become another person I have to watch. I can't do that and find her. You want to help? Stay here. Lean on Lane Fuller. Lean on Grant. Lean on every person who touched that call. You know how systems hide their mistakes. Make sure they can't hide this one."

Chase stared at him. For a second, Mark thought the man would tell him exactly where he could shove that.

Then Rose touched Chase's arm.

"Find her," she said to Mark.

Not please.

Not if you can.

Find her.

Mark nodded. "I will."

Rose held his gaze, and he had the unsettling feeling she could see right through every wall he had ever built. "And Detective?"

He stopped.

"She'll fight him," Rose said. "Whoever has her. She'll fight. So don't waste time thinking she'll wait quietly to be rescued."

For the first time since Chase and Rose had walked in, something like breath moved through Mark's chest.

Because that was Billy Jo.

Difficult. Stubborn. Mouthy. Brave in the way people were when they'd already survived too much and refused to be broken by one more man or woman with power.

"No," he said. "She won't."

Carmen grabbed her jacket from the back of her chair. "I'm still coming with you."

The chief looked as if he might argue, then didn't. "Both of you check in at each property. You find anything, you wait for backup."

Mark was already moving. "Sure."

"Mark."

He stopped at the door and looked back.

The chief's eyes narrowed. "I mean it. You don't go cowboy on this."

Mark thought of Billy Jo, alone somewhere, maybe tied up, maybe hurt, maybe furious and scared and waiting for someone to be smart enough to find her.

He pulled open the door.

"Then you'd better hope backup keeps up," he said, and stepped outside.

CHAPTER ELEVEN

ANOTHER HOUSE, ANOTHER PROPERTY. THIS ONE WITH lots of trees and bushes, maybe two to five acres. He could see four cars parked out front, a garden off to the side, and a group sitting around on lawn chairs on a patio in back.

He parked his Jeep behind a small blue Tracker and took in the pickup beside it just as Carmen pulled in behind him. Old. Gray, maybe blue once, with a dented tailgate and a right taillight cracked and taped over with red plastic. For a second, the detail tugged at him—something half-seen at the edge of the road earlier—but then Carmen's cruiser door opened, and the thought slipped.

"Stay," he said to the dog. He knew he could have left him at the station, but there was something about the dog disappearing the first time. He knew he may have gone after whoever it was who had been watching him. Dogs just had a way of picking up on things people missed. They read people better, too.

As he waited for Carmen to park and get out of the cruiser, a short, barefoot man in shorts was quickly heading their way.

Carmen closed her door. "You know what? I was halfway there and thought it might be best if we stuck together, watched each other's backs. We'll tackle this first and then head to the other."

He hadn't expected that, and he only nodded as the man approached.

"Hello there...!" He held up a beer, and Mark could see smoke trailing by the house from a barbecue.

"Hi. I'm Detective Mark Friessen. Do you own this place?" He took in the guy's dark, shoulder-length hair and the scraggly start of a beard. Carmen said nothing, and he didn't bother introducing her.

"No, I only rent it, me and my girlfriend. Is there something I can help you with?"

Mark scanned the single-story house with its dated, off-orange trim. The screen door was ripped, and rot marred the window frames. "And your name is?"

"Oh. I'm Shaun Carter. My girlfriend, Donna, and I live here. We just have some friends over for a barbecue. Was kind of worried for a minute that someone had complained."

Mark only nodded. "You get complaints? For what?"

The guy's gaze shifted from Mark to Carmen. "Not me, so to speak, but the guy who owns the place. It's a private road coming in here, and the cost is shared between six properties. The owner of this place puts nothing toward the annual project of fixing all the potholes and ruts. I know the lady at the end has really let me and Donna have it because we won't contribute. But as I told her, we only rent here. Covering that cost is the owner's responsibility. I figured you were here because of her. She is mighty pissed, and I can't blame her." He shrugged.

"Sorry, we don't handle those kinds of disputes," Mark said. "But since we're talking about your landlord, can you give us his name? We'd like to have a word with the owner of this property."

From his bugged-out expression, Mark suspected the guy was worried about something else. "Ah, sure... It's not a local guy. Some lawyer from California. I've got his number inside. He's kind of private. Is there something I should be worried about? Because Donna and I aren't too interested in moving right now..." He gestured behind him. Mark took a step and fell in beside him as they started walking toward the back, where people sat in lawn chairs.

"No, nothing like that. We're just following up on a situation the property owner may be involved in. You said he's a lawyer in California?" He took in two couples sitting on the old back patio, where the deck sagged and a support was gone. "How's it going?" he said to everyone.

They grew quiet, watching, a reaction he was used to when he showed up as a cop. People always stopped what they were doing.

"Uh...good," one of the guys said. He wore cut-offs and old runners, holding a beer. A girl in a sundress, hair pulled back, held tongs and turned hot dogs on an old gas barbecue.

"Donna, the cops here are looking for Fife's contact information," Shaun said.

Donna gestured to the open back door. "On the fridge. His card is stuck there, remember?"

Shaun stepped onto the concrete blocks that served as makeshift steps to the deck. "Don't step on that deck," he warned. "Fife isn't great at maintenance. That deck has been one step from someone breaking their neck since we moved here." He held the door open, and Mark followed him into a tiny, neat kitchen.

"Here it is." Shaun reached for a card stuck to the old yellow fridge—a color Mark didn't think they made anymore. He held it up, displaying a California number and email for a law firm: Fife Gattenburg. Mark added the information to his phone, noting the business name, Gattenburg and Associates.

"So, is there a problem with Fife?" Shaun asked. "I mean, we don't see him much. Only met him once. But he made it clear when he rented this to us that he wanted to make a profit. Kind of took that to mean not to call if something breaks. I know he's got a handyman he uses on the island, but..." Shaun didn't finish the thought.

Mark wasn't sure what to make of the comment. He took in the house around them. "Just a routine inquiry, but thanks for the number. I'll give him a call. You said he has a handyman on the island. Any idea who it is? And Fife, he owns a few places here on the island, right?"

From the face Shaun made, Mark didn't think he knew much about the owner. Or maybe it was something else. At least Mark had what he needed to get past the offshore company hiding the property's true ownership.

"I know he owns one other place," Shaun said. "Could be more, but for us, it's just about renting—not that you can be choosy. He doesn't bother us, and I only met his handyman once. Can't even remember his name..." He walked to the back door and called out, "Hey, Donna, you remember that weird guy who works for Fife? What's his name?"

"You mean Adam?" she said.

"You sure it was Adam?"

"Yeah, something like that. His name and number are in that drawer in the kitchen, I think."

Outside, Carmen was talking to one of the guys in a lawn chair, and Mark thought he heard him laugh at something she said.

Shaun opened a drawer overstuffed with paper and junk—the kind every kitchen had, holding things people didn't know what to do with. "Adam, Adam, Adam..." he muttered under his breath. "Donna said his number is in here somewhere." He started pulling things out.

Mark suspected this could take a while. "Tell you what, I have another stop to make. In the meantime, I'll call this Fife and ask him about Adam. I take it Adam lives on the island?"

Shaun, holding string, envelopes, and pencils, looked up. "I don't know exactly where he lives. Didn't ask. If I find his information, do you want me to call you?"

Mark reached into the pocket of his jean jacket and pulled out a card. "There's my cell. Just give me a call if you find it."

Shaun tacked the card on the fridge beside Fife's, and Mark headed out the door.

"Hey, smells good. Enjoy your barbecue," he called, gesturing to Carmen before starting back toward his Jeep. He heard their voices behind him. "I got the owner's number—some California lawyer. But a local guy is his handyman. I don't have his number, though."

"Well, interesting you should say that," Carmen replied. "As you were inside, after Donna called out his name—Adam —one of the guys on the patio asked if that was the same guy who does odd jobs around the island and drives that big old one-ton."

He paused by his Jeep, looking back at the young couples behind the old house, really taking it in. "You mean like the big rig that was parked off the road when I was there this morning?"

"Maybe, maybe not," Carmen said. "But he said it was gray, maybe blue once. Dented tailgate. Busted right taillight taped over with red plastic."

Mark felt something tighten low in his gut.

The truck beside the Tracker had that same taped taillight, but so had the flash of something he'd seen near the road earlier, or thought he'd seen. Red tape catching light. A dented tailgate. Gone before he could turn his head fully, before he'd known it mattered.

He looked back at the pickup parked in the yard. "That truck theirs?"

Carmen followed his gaze. "I already asked. Belongs to the guy in the cutoffs. Says it hasn't moved all afternoon."

Of course. One more almost. One more detail that could mean something or nothing.

She pulled open the door of her cruiser. "You got the number for the owner?"

"Right here." He held up his phone.

"Then call him while we drive to the other address he owns. I don't know, Mark, but sometimes this island and the people here..." She didn't finish.

"I know, Carmen. The secrets that seem to happen here are the kind that happen in too many places. What I don't understand is the note. Why? And why target Billy Jo?"

The way her gaze lingered, the way she pulled in a breath, it was as if she wanted to say something. She glanced away, then back to him. "If someone has it in for you, Mark, they'll go after who you care about to get to you."

He didn't want to hear this. He shook his head. "Billy Jo is just..."

"Okay, stop right there, Mark. I have two eyes, and I've seen you together," Carmen said. "I've been in the same room as you two. You may want to keep telling yourself you're not close, that you don't care, but this thing between you, we all see it. And whoever put that note on your Jeep evidently sees it too."

CHAPTER TWELVE

THE METAL DOOR CLANGED, AND BILLY JO SAT UP, blinking, from where she lay on her raincoat, her socks off. She'd drifted off in the heat. Her hand covered her face, the daylight blinding her for a moment after the darkness. Then came air, fresh air.

The man dumped two more bottles of water and a paper bag beside her. She could smell the burger, the fries.

"Hey, you know what?" she said. "I'd really like to use a bathroom, not a bucket or even an outhouse."

"And I'd like to have my sister back, but neither is going to happen," he said, his hand on the door. "Picked up a cheeseburger and fries. Even got you one of those apple turnover things."

She knew he was going to close the door again.

"Hey, wait! Don't go. I know this is about Mark. You're keeping me here to set a trap for him. But then what?"

His hair was a little raggedy; she wondered if he'd brushed it today or even yesterday. He had that messy look some guys had, making her wonder if they bothered with basic grooming. Sweat stains ran down the sides of his T-shirt, and his blue jeans were old and faded. The tattoo on his arm ran all the way down one side—a totem of some kind, from what she could figure: a bear, a snake, a knife.

"That's not your concern," he said. "You have food and water for being quiet. Keep it that way."

She crossed her legs, not bothering to get up, and crawled to retrieve the paper bag before returning to her spot. "I disagree. As you've pointed out, it's because Mark cares for me so much that I'm locked up. So what happens when he finds me? How do I get out of here? Are you planning to just let me go, or have Mark trade himself for me? You're not leaving me here to starve, so I'm wondering if you've thought this out. You must have a plan."

She opened the bag, her mouth watering at the savory scent. The water bottle was still by the door. She still didn't know this man's name, only that he had a sister, Whitney Chandler, who was now dead, and he blamed Mark for everything. Even she wished she could sit Mark down and find out what had really happened.

"Are you questioning my plan or trying to get in my head?"

She unwrapped the burger from its foil and took a bite. Hunger was hunger, and the coffeehouse sandwich, tuna, which she'd never liked, was still sitting there, untouched. "Kind of hard to get in your head when I don't even know your name. I'm just asking if you've thought this out. I mean, Mark comes looking, and then what?" She took another bite, watching him run his hand over the steel doorframe.

"Well, he's already looking for you. Even that chief and Deputy Zarko are looking. They found your car where I left it, so it's only a matter of time. But the thing is, he won't find you unless I want him to. And my plans for Mark aren't your concern."

An ache filled her chest. Mark could be walking right into

something that could end with him hurt or killed. "You know, as you've pointed out, Mark cares about me. I care about him, too. I get why you're angry. I'm furious for your sister and what happened to her, but at the same time, I know Mark, and you're blaming him for something that wasn't in his control."

There was something about her mouth. It had landed her in hot water too many times because she couldn't play the game of saying what someone wanted to hear.

"You don't know what you're talking about," he said. "Mark knew right from wrong, and standing down and looking the other way because you're told to doesn't give you a pass, Billy Jo. It doesn't make it right."

She lifted her gaze, chewed, then wrapped the rest of the burger and tucked it back in the paper bag. She wiped her hands together, considering the edge in his voice and the way he'd snapped at her.

"You think I don't understand anger and frustration?" she asked. "I grew up on the other side of that."

He made a low, dismissive sound. "You?"

"Yeah, me." She held his gaze, recognizing that familiar look—the one people got when they saw her now and thought they knew her story. "You talk about your family having nothing, but at least you had a family. Poor or not, I'd have given anything for that."

His hand remained on the door, but he didn't close it.

"My childhood years were spent being bounced from one home to the next," she said. "You're feeding me better than I ever ate in most of those places."

"You want me to feel sorry for you?"

"No. I want you to hear me." She leaned forward, feeling the heat of the metal floor through her jeans. "You think I don't get where you're coming from? I know very well what happened to you, to your sister. On the reservation, doors and services were closed to you. Even clinics there are staffed with doctors ordered to sterilize women without their knowledge."

His jaw tightened. "Don't talk like you know."

"I know enough," she said. "And I know the kind of depravity and evil that lurks in the men who do that, because I lived in houses with men like that."

Something shifted in his face.

Small.

There and gone.

Billy Jo saw it anyway.

"At night, I feared the evil that would walk into my room, into my bed—until my dad adopted me. He found me at a gas station when I pulled a gun on a man who would always get a pass, just like the oil worker who killed your sister."

He looked away first.

Not far. Just enough.

She had hit something.

"I lived it," she said. "I understand it. I still see their faces in my mind, feel the hate from being scared for so long because of what they did to me. You want to talk about a list of people to hate, to get even with, to get payback from? Let's compare. I wonder whose is longer."

Billy Jo was trembling. She didn't want that door to close one more time. There had to be a way to reach this man. Sharing her deepest, darkest horror stories was something she never did. She saw his surprise, as if he hadn't known.

"So you were...?"

"In foster care, born to a meth addict who tossed me away like I was garbage," she snapped.

The words cracked through the hot metal box.

He blinked.

For one second, he looked less like a man with a gun and a

plan, and more like someone who had heard something he understood too well.

"My mother..." he started, then stopped.

Billy Jo stilled.

There it was. A crack.

"What about your mother?" she said quietly.

His eyes hardened again. "Don't."

She hadn't meant for her anger to spill out, raw and ugly between them, but it was too late. He didn't know her past, the deep, dark places she'd clawed her way out of. "It's why I do what I do, why I showed up at your door to save a girl named Whitney. You think I don't understand why you're angry? I am angry for you—but this isn't the way."

"You don't get to tell me the way."

"No, maybe I don't," she conceded. "But I do get to tell you when you're aiming at the wrong person."

His lips twitched, that tell-tale tic again. "Mark Friessen is the wrong person?"

"He was a new deputy with no authority. His hands were likely tied in getting your sister the justice she deserved."

"He said she shouldn't have hitched."

"And if he said that, then he was an arrogant ass who deserved to be called out for it," Billy Jo said, watching his reaction.

He seemed surprised.

Good.

"But that doesn't make him the one who killed Whitney," she continued. "It doesn't make him the oil worker who walked away. It doesn't make him the sheriff who didn't care or the Feds who didn't show up."

He stepped into the container, just one step, big enough to block more of the light. "You think you can talk me out of this."

"No. I think you already know this won't bring her back."

His face went dark. "Don't say that."

"Why? Because it's true?"

"You don't know what I know."

"Then tell me," she urged. "Tell me your name. Tell me what really happened after Whitney died. Tell me what you did."

His gaze held hers, and for a moment she thought he might.

Then he looked toward the open doorway.

Not outside. Not exactly.

As if listening for something that wasn't there yet.

"Sure, I get the anger," Billy Jo said, her voice softer now, "but maybe you should focus that anger on who's really responsible: the Feds who don't give a damn, the policy-makers who create laws that keep people in poverty and steep this country deeper in inequality and elitism. How many girls did you say disappeared, twenty-five over how many years? Take a look at the numbers across the states, the country. If your sister hadn't been an Indian, her life would have mattered."

His eyes flashed.

"Don't pretty it up," he said.

"I'm not. I'm saying be angry at the people who built the system that made her disappear easy. Be angry at the policy-makers who've allowed cell phone companies to get away with not providing service in remote areas where privilege and wealth don't exist. Be angry at the laws that protect men with money and leave girls like Whitney on the side of the road."

He said nothing.

"So let's really talk about all the issues," she said. "The violence against women and children, the lack of quality housing, the poverty, the unemployment. Look how far your sister had to go for a job. And the services... She couldn't get a driver's license or training because of a lack of resources. We can talk about every inhumane thing that has happened to you, your sister, your mother, her parents, their daughters —everything they lacked, from real medical care to education, to clean water, to the ability to live without being hunted down and raped because the laws out there don't protect you. You think I don't know the bigger fight?"

She didn't know whether he was listening or truly hearing her. He just stood there, watching. She'd likely screwed herself by sharing too much and would never reach him now, because once hate took hold, sometimes a person couldn't be saved. Or maybe she could get him to stand down, to see reason.

"That's a nice speech for a white girl who seems to have landed on her feet."

So there it was. He was seeing her skin, not who she was.

She let out a sigh. "I guess you'd think that. Maybe that's part of the problem. You're looking at me and deciding what I am before you know anything about me."

His mouth tightened. "You don't know what that's like."

She laughed once, short and hard. "The hell I don't."

He stared at her.

"I'm sorry about what happened to your sister," she said. "It shouldn't have happened. But I do what I do for kids like her. Every fight I've had, as far back as I can remember, has been because I was looked down on, as if I were nothing. I know that feeling too well."

"You like to push, don't you?"

"I learned early that being quiet didn't save me."

That shut him up.

She reached into the paper bag and pulled out a fry, holding it up. "This here is pure heaven. Not something I ever had until I was out of jail. My dad and mom took me to my first drive-through. Now, you tell that to anyone and they think you're crazy. I mean, who hasn't been to a drive-through, had some fast food, a burger and fries...?"

From the way he was looking at her, she wondered if he believed her.

His gaze dropped to the fry, then to the bag, then back to her.

Something like shame passed over his face, and this time he didn't hide it fast enough.

"Not everyone has that, Billy Jo," he said. "We certainly didn't."

His voice was different. Lower. Less sharp.

"Then you get it," she said. "As a foster kid, in most of the places I lived, we never got that. That's the kind of thing you do for your kids when you care about them. It took me a long time to trust my parents. I still have to remind myself that my mom and dad care, that the rug isn't going to be yanked out from under me, that I am somebody."

He looked at the floor.

"What's your name?" she asked.

His gaze lifted.

She didn't push. Didn't breathe too loudly. Didn't move.

The silence stretched between them, thin and fragile.

"A—" he started.

Then he stopped.

Outside, somewhere beyond the barn, a low engine sound carried through the walls.

He heard it too.

Everything in him changed.

His shoulders tightened. His head turned toward the opening. The softness, if that was what it had been, vanished.

Billy Jo's stomach dropped.

No. Not yet.

"When I was in sixth grade," she said quickly, trying to pull him back, "one of my foster homes was this Christian family. They had a couple kids of their own. That was the first time I had religion shoved in my face—prayers before eating, Sunday church, Friday bible study, a Christian school that wouldn't allow a girl to wear pants."

He looked at her, but he was listening past her now.

"The school uniform was mandatory, with these ridiculous short skirts on girls," she said, faster. "That's likely why I hate dresses and skirts now. Boys would lift your skirt, and I hated it so much."

The engine cut off.

His eyes narrowed.

"One day I decided, nope," she said. "I left the house in pants without my foster mom seeing me. I walked into the school to voice my protest, so to speak. I was written up and sent home, because not only had I worn pants, but I'd also made a cardboard sign that said, 'You can't make me wear a skirt.' I stood on a desk and had a few of the other girls ready to join me when the teacher came in. The principal was called, and both my foster parents were there in the office, ordered to take me home because I was instigating a riot. I was eleven. By the end of the day, I was moved to a new foster home. Better? No, but at least I didn't have to wear a skirt."

She wondered if that was a smile he was fighting. He shook his head.

Then she heard something more clearly.

A car door.

She lifted her head, and he was in the container so fast, on her right as she opened her mouth.

"Help! In here..." was all she got out.

He had his hand over her mouth, holding her so tight she couldn't breathe. "Quiet," he whispered in her ear.

He was strong and sweaty. She clawed at his hand, but couldn't dislodge it. Her heart hammered. He reached for something with his free hand, and she fought, pushing at his arm as he shoved a piece of cloth into her mouth and yanked her hands behind her back.

He forced her to the ground, tying her fast as she tried to spit out the old-tasting rag. He knelt over her, yanking at her feet. She saw the rope on the floor as he bound her ankles so tightly it bit into her skin and burned.

Then he reached for her coat, ripping out the lining in a long strip. He rolled her over as she fought him, and he tied the strip around her mouth. She tried to yell and scream, but only muffled cries escaped. He kicked the paper bag holding her burger and fries to the side.

She heard another vehicle and knew someone else was there. As he stepped out of the container and held the door, she could barely move. She heard a door close.

"Hello?" a man called out.

She'd know that voice anywhere. She yelled, but gagged and tied, he'd never hear her. As the container door closed and locked, she knew Mark Friessen, the friend she cared too much for, was walking into a trap set by her captor.

She yelled and yelled against the cloth.

Please, please don't hurt him!

CHAPTER THIRTEEN

GETTING PEOPLE TO TAKE CALLS FROM A COP SEEMED almost impossible. Music played over the line as Mark drove to the other house owned by Fife Gattenburg. He'd called the law firm's business number and was now waiting for the lawyer to pick up.

"I'm sorry, Detective," the receptionist's voice was soft, almost a whisper. "Mr. Gattenburg isn't available. I'll have to take a message—and the reason for your call, if you don't mind."

Mark knew a brush-off when he heard one. Fife was likely standing right there. "Sure. As I said, this is Detective Mark Friessen, Roche Harbor Police. This is regarding an investigation and an incident at one of Mr. Gattenburg's properties. It's urgent. Please tell him I need him to call me back sooner rather than later. Stress the seriousness of this investigation." He still couldn't shake the feeling the lawyer had no intention of calling him back.

"I will give him the message."

Mark only shook his head. A breeze drifted through the open windows, and he glanced at his dog before lifting his gaze to the rearview mirror. Carmen was behind him, a plume of dust trailing her on the gravel road. How did so many parts of the island transition from super-rich, multimillion-dollar estates to places that looked slapped together by backwoods locals, nothing that would meet any building code?

His phone rang again as he slowed around a bend on a narrow, heavily treed road. He noted the office number and pressed the green answer button. "Detective Friessen," was all he said.

"Mark, just so you know, Chase McCabe is in Tolly's office, and he is not sitting quietly," Gail said.

Mark tightened his hand on the wheel. "That surprises no one."

"No, but he's demanding every detail of the investigation, and Tolly is doing that thing where he says less the louder someone gets. Rose is out here with me, staring at Billy Jo's phone as if she can will it to ring."

That hit harder than he expected. He looked through the windshield at the narrow road, overgrown branches scraping the side of his Jeep, and pictured Rose standing in the station, holding herself together because falling apart wouldn't find her daughter.

"Is Chase asking for me?" he said, though he already knew the answer.

"He asked where you went. I told him you and Carmen were following the property lead."

"Good."

"I'm not sure 'good' is the word I'd use," Gail said. "He looks like he's two seconds from commandeering Tolly's office and running the investigation himself."

Mark could believe that too. "Well, tell him if he wants to help, he can keep leaning on DCFS. Lane Fuller, Grant Webber—everyone who touched that intake call. Someone there missed something, or someone there knows more than they're saying."

There was a pause, and he could hear low, tense voices in the background.

"Already told him," Gail said. "He's making calls."

Of course he was.

"Well, I'm not sure how much you're going to share with him, but I found out the property is owned by a California lawyer by the name of Fife Gattenburg. He's the name behind that private company. I've called and left a message, but let's see if he calls back. I did speak with the tenants who rent the first house on Ryecraft, and they said there's a local caretaker named Adam who looks after the properties. They're supposed to call me back when they find out his last name, then you can run a check on him—and that lawyer, while you're at it. Carmen and I are on our way to the Hillcrest property together, so I'll let you know what I find. Anything else?" He thought she was writing this down.

"No, just call when you're done. I'll run a check on that lawyer. Tolly is still with Chase, and Rose is right here. They're not about to sit around and wait. They want answers about what happened to their daughter."

"Yeah," Mark said, taking in the bushes and what he thought was a driveway. "So do I."

"Got it," he said before he hung up. He pulled down the driveway, the dog panting, branches scraping his door. The ruts in the narrow dirt road had him wondering what was ahead.

As he rounded a bend, he spotted what looked like an old mobile home and a couple of sheds. He turned off his Jeep and unfastened his seatbelt as Carmen pulled in behind him.

"Stay in here," he said, then ran his hand over the mangy mutt he was rather fond of. He reached for his cell phone, pulled open his door, and stepped out.

Taking in the quiet, the overgrown grass, and patches of dirt, he looked for anything but saw nothing. "Hello?" he called out, unsure where to start. He tilted his head toward the dingy green and brown mobile home and started walking. "I'll try the trailer first."

Carmen only nodded and fell in behind him.

His cell phone rang. He spotted the name Shaun Cooper, from the house he'd just left. "Detective Friessen," he said, really feeling the remoteness of this place as he walked.

"Hey, Detective. Shaun here. I was just speaking with you about that caretaker. Well, I found his name. It's Adam Chandler. I have a cell phone number for him, too."

"Can you text it to me at this number?"

"Will do," Shaun said, then hung up.

Mark lifted his hand to Carmen, who was walking behind him, her hand on her holstered gun as if she expected something. That creepy feeling was back. "Adam Chandler is his name," he said. "What do you think the relationship is to Whitney Chandler, the girl Billy Jo was supposed to be picking up?"

He heard the ding and took in the number, holding his phone out to Carmen to show her—but his cell phone exploded in his hand.

There was a sharp crack, a flash of heat across his palm, and the phone kicked out of his grip in pieces. Plastic shards sprayed sideways. Something sliced across the inside of his hand, and a hot sting burned up his wrist. At the same time, Carmen's head snapped back as blood spurted across her face.

Everything happened so fast.

He pulled his gun and grabbed Carmen, who had gone down on the ground. He took in the blood oozing from her face, dragging her behind the trailer, holding one arm. His heart thumped, his breath loud in his ears. He felt exposed and didn't have a clue where that shot had come from.

"Carmen, you hit?"

She shut her eyes, a long blink, leaning against the rotted plywood skirting of the trailer. Blood ran over her eye. For a second, she said nothing. He looked around the corner, then squatted beside her, shaking her gently, seeing the shock, the stun, the gash in her head. He was looking for a bullet wound. She lifted her hand, wiping the blood with her shirt cuff so she could see.

"I'm okay," she said. "Just grazed me, I think. What the hell, Mark? Where did that come from?"

He scanned their surroundings but saw no one.

"Stop looking at me like I'm dead," she snapped, pressing her sleeve hard to her forehead. "It's a graze or a fragment. I can see, I can shoot, and I'm not bleeding out. Find the shooter."

That was Carmen. Bleeding, furious, and still thinking faster than most people standing upright.

"Can you call it in?"

She merely nodded. "Cell phone's in the car. I'll get it." She moved to stand, but he put a hand on her.

"No, I'll get it. You just sit there. Can you see? Can you point a gun?"

She grunted. "No, I'll go around the trailer. You call out and distract him. Just have my back."

He realized he didn't have a choice. He glanced toward the police cruiser and his Jeep. The dog appeared panicked, whining.

"Adam Chandler, this is Detective Mark Friessen," he shouted. "I just want to talk."

He glanced back at Carmen, who gestured to him from the other side of the trailer. Her gun was out, and she moved away from him, careful, fast, crouching through the brush. Mark listened for where he thought the shot had come from but heard nothing other than his dog barking.

When he looked over, the dog jumped out the passenger window and was running his way.

"Christ Almighty, dog, don't you dare get shot," he muttered, reaching for the dog and grabbing his collar. He dragged him around the corner, out of sight, because the last thing he wanted was his dog in the middle of a gunfight.

He didn't see Carmen anymore. The dog whined, nudging him, and he took in the blood on his hand. A shot fired, and a bullet ricocheted right above his head at the corner of the trailer. He flattened against the wall, holding the dog's collar as he growled. He knew he wanted to race over there. His heart was slamming in his chest, and he had to remind himself to breathe.

"You stay. Down," he said, his voice low, but the dog stayed. "Shh," he said again when the dog whined and looked up at him.

There was no way in hell he'd watch his dog take a bullet. He peered around again, listening for whoever was out there. Carmen would be working her way to her cruiser, which was right out in the open.

He spotted the sheds, the trees. "Hey, I know you're out there," he called. "You left that note on my Jeep, Adam. You have Billy Jo McCabe. She has nothing to do with this. You have an issue with me—that note made that clear—so let's deal with it. I'm right here. Come out. Let's talk about this, man to man."

Another bullet ricocheted just above his head. He ducked, feeling the splinter of wood bite into his cheek. It felt wet. He swiped at it, seeing blood on his hand.

"Shh, shh, stay," he told the dog again, who lay down this time. Mark looked around, spotting one of the old sheds. He needed to find a way to get over there. "Adam, I don't know what this is about, but if you have an axe to grind with me, come out and talk."

He crouched, taking in the bushes, the trees. He figured he could run maybe thirty feet to get behind a large tree. Whoever this guy was, he was good at staying hidden.

Mark was up and running, crouching low. Bullets fired at his feet as he pounded the ground and dove behind the tree. He peered around, then ran again. The shots were coming from the other side of what looked like an old hay shed or a small barn. He held his gun, glancing back. The dog had stayed put.

This guy hadn't said a word. This was a game he didn't like.

"Adam, look! I'm here now. You have Billy Jo. Where is she? I need you to let her go."

He heard shots again but knew by the sound that they'd hit the side of the cruiser or his Jeep. He moved around the side of the shed, which was bigger than he'd thought, keeping his back to the warped wood.

He reached an old sliding door and pushed it open, peering into the kind of place where a man could hide and shoot him without warning. He crouched low. Around the corner, in the dim light, lay old farm tools, broken windows, and a metal cargo container. He moved to an old stall, where he could see out through a crack in the wood.

A faint bang echoed, and he dragged his gaze to the container, praying Carmen had reached her phone and was calling for help. He crept toward the metal container, his eyes on the door.

"Hey, anyone in there?" he called out.

Another bang, this time from inside. He rushed to the front, spotted the handle, and pulled. The door clanged open, revealing only darkness. Someone lay tied on her side, bare feet kicking the wall.

"Billy Jo..."

The moment he saw her, her wide, panicked eyes met his

from behind the gag. She was yelling, struggling against her bonds.

"I'll get you out of here," he said, stepping onto the threshold, his hand still on the door.

A hard metal press against the back of his head, then a click.

"Now that was easy," a voice said from behind him.

He knew this had to be the man behind the note. "Adam Chandler?" he asked.

Billy Jo struggled, helpless in her ties. A hand reached for his gun and took it.

"So you figured it out. But I wonder, Mark Friessen, if you actually remember who I am."

He didn't pull his gaze from Billy Jo, who continued to strain against the gag.

"Whatever it is, Adam, this isn't going to solve anything."

Adam Chandler, Adam Chandler... He repeated the name in his head, searching his mental list, knowing one wrong word could end badly for both of them.

Then he remembered the name, the face—a family that had been screwed over.

"Get in," Adam said to Mark.

He felt the hand on his back. One foot was on the container floor, the other on the ground, his hands in the air. The way Billy Jo looked at him screamed, *Don't get in*.

"First, why don't you tell me what you want from me, Adam? The note said payback. Maybe you should tell me what that means, what your price is. Or is it my life?" he said, unable to tear his gaze from Billy Jo. She was scared, freaked out, pleading with him.

"Well, let's talk about that, Mark," Adam said. "Imagine twenty-five girls disappear, vanish. Some are found dead, others not. If this happens in suburbia, white girls with parents whose jobs matter, who have money, then you have city police officers on the case. A hunt for a serial killer is declared. Law enforcement are pulled in from the county, and the Feds lend their support. You'd have overtime, every resource available. The city and county would be shut down while you hunted and found that killer. You'd turn over every rock until he was found, no resources spared. But imagine now that those twenty-five girls aren't white. They don't have addresses that matter. They're just Indians on res land. What happens then, Mark?"

He didn't want to answer, knowing he hadn't gotten through. "Their cases get buried, closed," he said. "If time allows, a detective might make a few calls. No interagency resources are allocated. The girl is likely labeled a runaway, a sex worker—someone the county, state, and Feds won't waste time on. Nothing is shut down—not the city, the county, or the reservation. Is that what you want to hear? Because I'll say it. I'll admit it happens, and it's not right. But ask yourself this, Adam: You want payback from me, but shouldn't you be asking where this comes from? Not from me, who's ordered to look away. Not even from my boss. It's his boss's boss who directs where resources go, which cases to investigate, which ones to file away."

Billy Jo was quiet, staring in horror, but the truth was the truth. Mark knew he was going to end up with a bullet in his head, but he needed to get Billy Jo out of there.

"Get on your knees," Adam said, pressing the cold steel of the gun into the back of Mark's head.

"Look, this isn't the way. Let Billy Jo go. You've got me..."

He felt a sharp blow to the back of his head and thought he heard a gunshot. Billy Jo went fuzzy in front of him, slowly, slowly. What she was yelling, he couldn't make out. The room spun, the light dimmed, and then he felt nothing.

CHAPTER FOURTEEN

THE CONTAINER DOOR WAS OPEN. MARK LAY FACE DOWN where he'd fallen after the man he'd called Adam hit him hard with the butt of his gun. Someone had fired a shot at the man who'd locked her up, tied her up, and terrorized her. He was no longer standing in the doorway, and all she could do as she struggled was stare in horror at an unmoving Mark.

"Damn you, Mark! Don't be dead!" she screamed at him from behind her gag, digging her toes into the steel wall and rolling onto her side to squirm her way toward him.

"Wake up, Mark!" Her voice was muffled, but she kept trying to rub off the gag. Adam had tied it too tight. He was good at it. There was no give in the ropes, so tight they bit into her skin as she fought, straining, pulling, and yanking. She didn't care if she was bleeding, didn't care about the rawness or the bite of pain. She only moved, willing Mark to move, to moan, to do something so she could see he was alive.

She kept going, slithering and writhing until she lay beside him. She managed to slide around and bump him, nudging his leg with her feet, feeling the hard muscle. "Mark, wake up," she called through the gag.

She heard him stir and kept kicking and nudging until he moved.

"Ah, fuck, what happened?" he bit out.

She'd never thought his voice could be the sweetest sound. For a moment, she turned her head, her chest tightening as she fought the urge to weep. Damn him. Damn her. She didn't cry. She wouldn't.

He pushed up on an arm, shook his head, then blinked. His hand found her arm, helping her struggle to a sitting position. His fingers slid down her arm, reaching for the gag. He stared at her with those vibrant blue eyes she still couldn't shake from her dreams. He yanked the gag from her mouth, leaving it hanging around her neck.

"Untie me," she said. "Are you okay?"

He was on his knees, fighting the effects of blacking out. He wasn't okay. He touched his head, squeezing his eyes shut for a moment. "Shit... What happened?"

"He hit you with his gun. Someone shot at him. Come on, we have to get out of here. Untie me, help me..."

Mark reached behind her, pulling at the rope's knots, then drew a pocketknife from his jacket. "Hold still," was all he said, sliding the knife into the ropes and cutting them. Her hands were free.

She sat up, pulling the torn coat lining from around her neck as Mark cut the rope binding her ankles and yanked it away.

"Move your hands. Let me," he said when her fingers couldn't dig in to untie the knot. He reached around her with the knife, cutting through it. Her hand went to his chest, feeling the solid wall of him.

He pulled the cloth away and tossed it aside, then struggled to his feet, staggering slightly. Her feet were bare as she placed her hands on the steel floor and stood, her hand going to his arm. He leaned over, resting his hands on his knees, shaking his head again. Then he straightened, looking too much like a tall, rugged cowboy. He shouldn't have looked so good.

"Are you okay? You're not going to pass out, are you?" she asked, still holding his arm. She couldn't stop trembling as he pulled away, glancing out of the cargo container.

He'd already stepped down in those cowboy boots. "Come on, get down," he said. "We have to get out of here." He held out his hand impatiently, and she took it, feeling his strength.

He helped her down just as she heard another pop, pop of a gunshot. She went down, his body covering hers, grinding her face into the dirt.

"Fuck, Mark, get off," she hissed, but he was already dragging her by her shirt, then her pants, then her arm, pulling her toward the door.

She didn't know where to look. Would bullets fly? Would that crazed, angry man appear? "Who's shooting, Mark?" she asked, barely getting her feet under her as she stopped at the door and crouched.

The dog raced in, nudged Mark, then licked both their faces.

"I told you to stay," Mark muttered.

She heard the anger in his voice. She put a hand on the dog as Mark pulled up his pant leg, reaching for a gun tucked in the ankle holster of his boot.

He glanced at her, then down. "You're barefoot..." he started.

Another shot rang out. Mark ducked. So did she, then glanced at the cargo container, with no intention of going back for the boots she'd kicked off.

He grabbed her hand before she could speak. "Stay

behind me. Has to be Carmen out there. Good, she's okay." His voice was abrupt as he looked out the door, gun drawn.

Billy Jo reached for the dog's collar with her free hand to hold him back. Mark let go of her hand, glancing back at her.

"You okay?" he asked. There it was—a second of concern. No time now. They would have time later to check for bumps and scrapes, to take stock of what the hell had just happened.

"I'll be better when we get out of here," she said, a snarl under her breath.

He nodded, glancing at her feet again. "Keep up and stay behind me. Let's go."

He slipped out and hurried into the brush just outside the old outbuilding. Stepping on twigs and walking as quietly as she could, she followed him on a path away from the shed. Rocks and pebbles jabbed into the bottoms of her feet. She winced, struggling to keep up, wanting to shout.

She let go of the dog when she stumbled, feeling a thorn pierce her foot. The dog raced past Mark. He glanced back at her, down at her bare feet, seeing her limp.

"Get on my back," he told her.

She put a hand on him for balance and lifted her foot to pull out the thorn, seeing the scrapes. She realized he was serious as he crouched down. "You want me to get on your back—as in...?"

"For fuck's sake, Billy Jo. There's a crazy guy with a gun back there. Get on. We'll argue later. You're barefoot and can barely keep up."

At his sharp tone, she wanted to argue, but he reached for her hand, pulled her over, and she wrapped her arms around his shoulders, climbing onto his back. He tucked his gun into his waistband, then stood, his hands gripping her legs. She straddled him, a man she'd never been this close to, and held on as he hurried down the path.

He ducked under the branch she brushed away. The trees opened into long grass and a field. She saw the dog sniffing.

"Dog, come here," Mark said in a low voice.

Billy Jo looked around, holding tight. "He's going to kill you, Mark. There is no Whitney Chandler anymore," she whispered into his ear. His red hair was so short, the soft, natural curls begging to be touched. He shifted her in his arms. She knew she was heavy, and the position was damn uncomfortable.

"Carmen was trying to get to her phone in the cruiser when he pinned us behind the trailer. I thought he was hiding back by the outbuildings. She was hurt. I'm going to get you to the road, then I've got to go back for her."

He was going to leave her. Maybe that's why she tightened her grip around his neck. He reached up, gripping her arm. There was no way she was letting him walk back in there alone.

"You're not leaving me. I'm going with you."

He shook his head, letting her legs go. She slid down. He still held her arm, then squatted, reaching for the dog as it ran back to them. "No, Billy Jo, listen to me. I need you to get the dog out of here. I'll get you over to the road. It's not far. Damn, sometimes I wish this part of the island wasn't so isolated. You don't know anyone over here?"

She had no clue where she was. She looked up at him, at his red hair, the arrogant set of his jaw. She didn't think she'd ever get over it if he was shot, if he was killed. "I have no fucking idea where we are. I drove in and parked, and..."

He shook his head. "That was across the island. He apparently moved you. You don't remember?"

She shook her head. "Oh, great. No, of course not. He knocked me out. Propofol, he said. I woke up in the container and just figured..." She frowned. She didn't remember any of it.

He didn't pull his gaze from her. The way he looked at her, really looked, made her want to hide. He knew her better than she allowed anyone to.

"Mark, you know who that guy is? You called him Adam."

The face he made revealed the weight he carried.

"Mark, what happened? This is about his sister, from the little I got him to say. Is it true, what happened to her? And no one bothered looking for her...?"

The answer was etched on his face. She knew Mark better than she wanted to. "He has a right to be angry, but this..." He only shook his head, pulling a hand over his face.

She couldn't look away. "So he was right. Mark, did you look the other way?"

There was a side of Mark she was beginning to understand. He never explained himself, and she saw it now. Right or wrong, he carried a weight she understood too well.

"I've got to get back to Carmen. Take this," he said, pulling his gun from his waistband and holding it out.

She stared in horror, shaking her head, but he grabbed her hand roughly and pressed the gun into it.

"Take the damn gun! You stay low and head for the road that way. Keep the dog with you. If you see him, Adam, you shoot. An angry man with an axe to grind with me isn't going to hesitate to shoot you at this point." He pressed his hands to her face.

Still shaking her head, staring at the gun he'd forced on her, she reached for his arm, grabbing the hem of his jean jacket. She took in the man she didn't want to care for. "Mark, I don't need the gun. You take it. It's you he wants, not me. I'm just bait..."

But he lifted a finger to his lips. She wasn't sure why, as if he'd heard something, the way he stared at her. Then the dog growled and snapped. Mark tried to reach for him, but everything moved in slow motion again.

Mark went sideways, tackled by Adam, who dove out of the bush. They were punching, fighting on the ground, rolling in the field. She could see a struggle for the gun between them. The dog was snapping and biting at Adam as he fought Mark.

Billy Jo lifted the gun in her hand, trembling. "Mark!" she yelled.

She tried to aim, but Mark and Adam were rolling too fast, a tangle of arms and legs and rage. One wrong pull and she could hit Mark. Her hands shook so hard the gun felt alive in them.

"Damn it," she hissed, backing one step, then another, trying to find a clear line.

The dog lunged again, teeth flashing, and Adam snarled as he twisted beneath Mark. Billy Jo saw Adam's hand shift, saw the barrel of his gun swing away from Mark and toward the dog.

No.

"Adam!" she screamed.

He looked at her.

One second. Not even that.

But it was enough for Mark to drive his elbow up, hard, catching Adam under the jaw. The gun jerked. Billy Jo squeezed the grip tighter, trying to steady her aim, but the shot cracked before she could fire.

A pop, pop—a gunshot. She heard the dog yelp, and her heart dropped to her toes.

Carmen raced out of the bush. "Get down, get off!" she yelled, pulling Adam off Mark, pressing her gun to the back of his head.

Mark scrambled out from under him. "No, no, no... Please, no!" he cried, crawling to the dog, who lay in the grass.

In that second, all she saw was the blood on Carmen's

shirt, Adam with his hands cuffed behind him, and Mark holding the dog.

CHAPTER FIFTEEN

He was running, pounding the ground in his cowboy boots. "Don't you dare die, do you hear me? Stay with me. I swear to God, dog, what the hell were you thinking...?" He could see his Jeep. Billy Jo was behind him, running barefoot, a mess of sweat and dirt. His heart was breaking because the dog was bleeding. He knew the bullet was still in there. He wanted to kill that man with his bare hands; his dog had been trying to save him.

"Go, go!" Billy Jo yelled. "Is he breathing? How is he?"

"Stay with me," he said to the dog, struggling to hold him. The dog whimpered, and Mark feared he'd never make it.

Billy Jo was right behind him when he reached the Jeep. "Put him on my lap, Mark," she yelled, scrambling into the passenger side. He slid the dog onto her lap and yanked off his jean jacket to press it to the wound.

"Go, drive! I've got it," she yelled, pulling the jacket over the dog's side.

"Can you see where he's hit?" he yelled, jumping behind the wheel, the keys still in the ignition. He cranked the engine, backed out, and floored it over the ruts, the Jeep going sideways.

"I don't know, Mark. His side, around his belly. I don't know dog anatomy! He's bleeding a lot..."

Mark flew out of the driveway just as the chief's car pulled up. He barely missed it, blasting the horn without stopping, grinding the gears, his foot shaking.

Billy Jo murmured, "You're going to be okay. Come on, that's a good boy... Mark, hurry."

He took in his speed, close to seventy on the narrow gravel road. He blasted his horn just before the bend to warn anyone coming his way and took the corner faster than he should have.

"Hang on!" he shouted. "Come on, dog, don't you dare die on me. Come on!"

There were miles to town, and he felt a life he couldn't lose slipping from him. He swerved onto the main road behind a compact car doing forty, blasted his horn, and accelerated around it, tires squealing on the blacktop.

"Billy Jo, how's he doing? Don't let him die."

"Just drive, Mark. Get us there, hurry!"

He pressed the gas, the edge of town blurring past. The vet was three blocks from the station. He leaned on the horn through a four-way stop, swerving around three cars. When an SUV wouldn't move, he drove up the wrong side of the road, horns blaring at him, but all he could see was the vet's sign.

He laid on the horn, crossing both lanes of traffic into the gravel lot, then slammed the brakes, skidding to a stop. The clinic door opened, and someone stepped out. Billy Jo had already opened the passenger door and slid out. He took in his jean jacket, soaked with blood.

He scooped up his dog, nearly losing his balance as he ran around the front of the Jeep. He stumbled, hitting the front of the vehicle with his arm, and saw the vet and the assistant who worked the desk.

"He's been shot! My dog's been shot!" was all he could manage as he regained his feet and ran up the steps. The door was held open for him.

"Down here! Bring him down here," the vet called, a big, balding man in a dress shirt and blue jeans, a stethoscope around his neck. He tapped a table. "Put him here."

Mark laid his dog on the steel table. The vet opened a cupboard, grabbed a syringe, and filled it. The vet assistant quickly placed an IV in the dog's leg.

Mark moved to his dog's head, petting him, kissing him. "Don't you dare check out on me," he murmured, seeing the dog's closed eyes, his labored breathing.

"Mark, go to the waiting room," the vet said. "I need to get an x-ray, find out where the bullet is. Trudy!" he called, then lifted the dog and the IV bag in his arms and hurried out of the room.

Mark stood there, taking in the blood on his shirt, his hands. Billy Jo stood in the open doorway, barefoot, blood covering her dirty sweatshirt. She walked into the room, and Mark choked on a sob. He stood by the table, a tightness in his chest. His eyes burned as he looked up and felt her hand on his chest.

Then she slid her arms around him, holding him tight. He pulled her closer, squeezing his eyes against the dampness that pricked them. He pressed a kiss to the top of her head.

"It's going to be okay, Mark," she finally said, her hand rubbing his back. She didn't move, giving him a moment to compose himself. He never cried. When she finally stepped back, her hand remained on his arm. She looked away, granting him a second of dignity as he roughly swiped a hand across his wet face.

He tried to take a step, but his legs felt weak. Billy Jo's

hand was still on his back, rubbing. He cleared his throat roughly, resting his hand on the steel table, his gaze falling on the drops of blood from his mangy mutt.

"Let's go sit in the waiting room," she said. "You need someone to look at your head. You were out cold for a few seconds. You're probably still dizzy, shaky..."

He knew what she was doing—trying to distract him, being the kind of friend he didn't understand why he couldn't just be okay with. They walked down the hall to the waiting room.

"And you're still barefoot," he said. "You need to get yourself looked at, too. How are you, anyway? I didn't get a chance to ask."

Billy Jo gestured to the empty chairs. He didn't want to sit but knew he needed to. He sat, his long legs splayed, and leaned forward, resting his forearms on his thighs. He felt her hand on his shoulder, rubbing, as she stood beside him. They were a sight, both of them.

She sat next to him, and he glanced over. Her expression lacked the attitude he'd come to expect. She didn't smile, either, and he was grateful for that. "I just need a hot shower, some food. Coffee would be great. My feet..." She lifted one foot, crossing it over her knee to pull a pebble from the sole. He saw scrapes and rawness, dirt and grit, but she wasn't falling apart. She was so damn tough.

"What happened? Why didn't you call me?" he said. "You should have called before you went to that house, into a situation like that. That was really stupid, Billy Jo." He hadn't meant to sound so accusing. He hadn't even planned to ask.

She looked away, narrowed her gaze, and shrugged. What that meant, he didn't know. "It was late. The call was from a man I'd never heard from before. Honestly, I thought about calling you, but I didn't. So, who called me? I guess it wasn't someone filling in for Grant. I didn't find out everything from

—Adam Chandler, so that was his name? You don't have to rub salt in the wound, Mark. I know it was stupid. It was just..." She shrugged.

It wasn't lost on him that she'd never really answered. She was the most unforthcoming woman he'd ever met, bottling everything up better than he did.

"You got a call from Lane Fuller at DCFS, only he didn't know where the call had come from. Grant had no idea who Lane Fuller was. My last call to them, I think they were trying to figure out where the complaint originated, why the miscommunication, or who to blame for their screw-up."

She pursed her lips and shook her head—pissed, he thought. "Wow, it's amazing how screw-ups happen. Grant didn't tell me he was going to be away..."

"I think that was also part of the problem," Mark said. "He wasn't. He said he doesn't know Lane Fuller. It sounds as if there was confusion in the ranks."

Billy Jo made a rude noise. "That's putting it mildly. You know, I got into this to make a difference, but the red tape, the mismanagement, the rules that make no sense, the double talk, the decisions based only on paper, the mistakes that are ignored... People make decisions for kids without having a clue of the challenges they face, and your hands are tied when you try to do the right thing. Is that what happened to you with his sister, Whitney?"

He didn't look away from Billy Jo. If it were anyone else, he probably wouldn't have answered. But there was just something about talking to her. He knew she understood things no one else would.

He shook his head, still leaning over, her hand on his back. He stared at her dirty feet, knowing she'd run barefoot over everything for his dog, for him. He fisted his hand and pressed it to his forehead, rubbing for a minute.

"Whitney Chandler worked at a truck stop restaurant

twenty miles from her home. She had to hitchhike to get there from the reservation. She had a mother, a grandmother, and a brother. When the res police called the sheriff, you know what he said? He leaned out the door, because he was handling something else, having a bottle of bourbon with the lead deputy, I think. It was a gift that had been dropped off earlier. He just walked over, glass still in hand, and said, 'There's another Indian girl missing, Mark. Go on out there. The res police are there, but it's just as likely she up and left for something better.'"

"I thought he was joking. He wasn't politically correct about a lot of things. I was so proud of my gun, my badge—so arrogant. I was doing what I wanted, and I figured I'd handle it. I'd fix it. So I drove out to the res. Driving in, I saw the poverty. I stepped out and walked up to the door, taking in the rundown singlewide trailer, full of people—the mother and grandmother with friends, some outside, some in the kitchen, some in the living room. Everyone was just sitting, waiting for a phone to ring or something.

"I didn't have a clue what to do. For a second, everyone looked at me, and I knew I was in over my head. I talked to the res police who were there, and they had less than nothing to work with. I drove to the truck stop. She'd shown up for work, and when she left, the cook said he saw her hitching a ride home. That was the last time anyone saw her. No idea who picked her up.

"I figured the sheriff would want to know. I started looking into it, did up a report, and was sitting at my desk, typing it up when he asked me what I was doing. I gestured to the report about the missing girl, filling him in. The way he looked at me, then over to one of the senior deputies, I thought they'd start a search and find her. But it was handed over to a cop who closed it before it was even opened. He said she'd run off and was likely working the truck stops, selling herself.

"Her brother, Adam, called every day, and so did her mother. The res police couldn't do anything. Then, her things were found at one of the main camps off yonder that was building pipelines. I hated those places—always trouble with them, the crime, the booze, the drugs, the problems..."

He shook his head. Her hand was still on his back, and he saw by the way she knit her brows together that she understood. "One of the grunts working the line, the one who had her things, was arrested. But as one of the deputies walked him through the station door, the sheriff walked right out of his office and unlocked his cuffs, said he was free to go. A call had come in. I stood there, wondering what the fuck had just happened.

"A company SUV from the camp pulled up, and he got in. The sheriff said his hands were tied, that we weren't pursuing it. He wouldn't rattle the cage of the big oil company that owned that camp. The case was closed. I heard the oil worker left the next day, sent somewhere else by the company. I was assigned with telling the family the party line, that the case was closed but we'd keep looking, blah, blah, blah. She was just another girl no one would be looking for."

"Mark." Billy Jo tapped his arm, and he looked up to see the vet assistant walking straight toward him.

He stood up and took a step toward her, his stomach knotting from the seriousness on her face. "No, please..."

"He's lost a lot of blood, Mark, but we got the bullet out. The doctor is just stitching him up. Then it's a matter of wait and see. He'll be out to talk to you. Then you should go home; we'll call."

Billy Jo smacked his arm. "That's good news, Mark."

He only nodded and shut his eyes for a second. "Thank you. Just do whatever you have to do to save him."

As the vet assistant hurried back down the hall, Billy Jo's hand slipped from his arm.

Only then did she look down at her hands. They were still curled as if she were holding him, though Lucky was gone. Blood had dried in the lines of her palms and under her nails. Mark's jacket. Lucky's blood. Maybe some of hers. She couldn't tell anymore.

She tried to open her fingers, but they wouldn't move.

For a second, the waiting room tilted. The tile floor, the chairs, the smell of antiseptic, wet dog, and blood all blurred together. She was back in that steel box, heat pressing down on her, rope biting her wrists, cloth in her mouth, Mark not moving on the floor.

She sucked in a breath too fast.

Not here. Not now.

She forced one finger open, then another. The skin pulled where the blood had dried. Her knees went soft, and she locked them hard. Mark was standing right there, looking as if one more thing might break him.

He didn't need her breaking too.

Not yet.

He pulled Billy Jo into his arms and hugged her again.

CHAPTER SIXTEEN

"Mark... Mark, no! Don't go back there," Gail said.

She and Carmen were in his face the minute he stepped through the front door of the station, digging into each step. It was likely the murderous rage he knew was on his face that had them jumping in front of him, both women trying to stop him as he kept moving to the door where the cells were, where he knew Adam would be sitting.

He wasn't going to be stopped by anyone.

"Get out of my way," he grated, a furious, ugly emotion festering deep inside him, making him want to punch something. He'd never expected to be here again.

The fluorescent lights overhead buzzed, too bright, a harsh counterpoint to Gail's voice, Carmen's sharp breath, and the blood still rushing in his ears. He smelled himself: sweat, dirt, and blood. Lucky's blood. Maybe his own. Maybe Billy Jo's.

"You're not going back there, not like this," Gail said, her voice loud and demanding. "For the love of God, Mark, look at you. You're a mess. Go home."

Carmen stood beside her, a bandage on her forehead

where the bullet had grazed her. He hadn't even asked how she was. Her face was pale beneath dried blood they hadn't quite cleaned away, but her eyes were steady on his, and that somehow made him feel worse.

"Mark!" the chief called out.

He stopped, dragging his gaze to the chief standing in his office doorway. Adrenaline still pulsed through him, making his chest heave. He said nothing, just stared, breathing in, breathing out, clenching and unclenching his fists at his sides. Gail and Carmen watched him, and he knew they'd never seen him like this.

"How's the dog?" the chief asked.

He pulled in another breath and lifted a dirty, bloody hand, raking it over his face. He could hear the scrape of whiskers. "They got the bullet out, but he lost a lot of blood. We wait and see." He willed the dog to pull through, remembering Lucky in the cage, asleep, a big bandage around him, and the unexpected ache in his heart.

"You see a doctor about your head?" the chief pressed. "Heard you took a big knock from Chandler."

Mark could see the door to the back, but Gail remained directly in front of him. She dropped her hand from his chest, where she'd been holding him back, and crossed her arms. He'd have to physically move her to get past.

"No, I'm fine..." he started.

The chief hadn't pulled his hard gaze from him. Mark had no idea what he was thinking. "You're not fine. No one here is. Did the McCabe girl get home okay?"

He saw what this was—a distraction. Next, the chief would have him turned around and out the door. "Chase and Rose picked her up from the vet clinic. She wanted to go home, but I think they were stopping at the hospital first."

They were fussing over Billy Jo, doing the parent thing she hated. From the look in her father's eye, Mark knew he understood everything that could have gone wrong. He should have said something more to them.

"We need a statement from her, and you too," the chief said. "Get your paperwork done after you go home and get cleaned up. Get some food in you, and get a doctor to look at your head."

Mark didn't nod, but he made a face. There was no way he was turning around and walking out that door. "Fair enough, but I'm talking to him." He jabbed his hand toward the door to the cells.

The chief glanced at Gail as if acknowledging they'd have to drag Mark out of there.

Of course, Mark hadn't planned it further than this.

"Let him back there," the chief said, then nodded and dragged his gaze back to Mark. "But you pull it together. You're running hot, and I'm not having that here."

Mark heard the warning. "Got it. But this is personal."

Gail stepped back but didn't pull her gaze from him, then rested her hand on his shoulder and patted it. "You need another minute, Mark?"

He only shook his head, feeling the stubbornness in him. "I'm good."

The chief only nodded, then stepped back into his office, but not before glancing back at him once more. "Mark, I get it, but personal or not, I'm not having you stir something up here so his lawyer has something to use. He's been questioned and has asked for a lawyer. Tread carefully..."

Then the chief closed the door.

Mark took in the cells ahead, wiping his hand over his face.

"You just need a few days, Mark. Take them," Gail said, rubbing his shoulder again.

He said nothing else as he took one step, then another, his hand finding the door. The metal was cool under his palm.

For a second, he just stood there, breathing through the burn in his chest, the throb in the back of his skull, the image of Lucky lying in Billy Jo's lap, his blood soaking through Mark's jacket.

Then he opened the door and stepped in.

The sound changed the second the door closed behind him. The station noise dropped away, replaced by the low buzz of fluorescent lights, the hum of old pipes, the faint metallic clink from the end cell. The back hallway smelled of disinfectant, stale coffee, concrete, and something else underneath—sweat and fear ground into old walls.

The cells were empty except for the one on the end.

Mark strode past the first two, his boots loud on the floor. Too loud. Each step seemed to echo back at him.

Then he saw him: dark hair, shaggy beard, lying on a cot against the wall, one knee up, an arm resting over it. His wrists were cuffed in front, the chain resting against his thigh. Dark eyes tracked Mark until he stood on the other side of the bars, looking in.

Mark didn't have a key, which was a good thing. He stared back, feeling anger resonate, knowing this man, given access and opportunity, wouldn't hesitate to kill him.

He leaned against the bars, saying nothing for a minute.

Adam didn't move.

Neither did Mark.

The silence stretched thin, broken only by the fluorescent hum and the small shift of Adam's cuffs when he flexed his hands.

"You shot my dog," Mark finally snapped.

Adam didn't look away, but he didn't speak.

Mark's fingers curled around the bars, feeling the grit of old paint under his palm. "You must really hate me to go to the lengths you did—watching me, digging into my life and the people in it. To put in motion what you did, calling Child

Services so Billy Jo would show up on your doorstep..." He pulled in a breath, but it did nothing to cool the rage under his ribs. "She's a woman who helps girls like your sister. You didn't make it easy, finding her. Would you have killed her?"

Adam pulled in a breath, as if he might not answer, then gestured toward Mark. "This wasn't about her. I knew you'd come looking. Been watching you for a while."

Mark only nodded, then repeated, "Would you have killed her?"

Something about the man's cold-blooded anger made it clear the lines had blurred for him. "Pretty sure I asked for a lawyer. Not talking."

Mark gritted his teeth and kicked at some dust on the floor with his cowboy boot. The dust skittered across the concrete and stopped against the bars.

"When I showed up at your door, when the sheriff sent me because your sister went missing, the minute I walked in, I knew I was in over my head. I never understood why the sheriff sent me, not at first. Oh, sure, I was new, excited for a big case, thinking he trusted me because he saw something in me. What a fool I was for believing that."

Adam's gaze didn't change, but his cuffed hands went still.

"I didn't have a clue what to do," Mark said. "I went to the truck stop restaurant where Whitney worked, where she'd hitchhiked home. I can't imagine that. Maybe I wondered what kind of people let their daughter hitchhike on a highway where cell service disappears the closer you get to the reservation. The res police have no resources. Their only jurisdiction is the res, and where she worked wasn't on it. That was the county, the sheriff I worked for. When her body was found on res land, dead, assaulted, brutalized..."

He stopped.

The words sat there, ugly and heavy.

Adam looked older now, but Mark tried to remember how

old he'd been when he first walked into that rundown trailer and saw their anguish. Barely shaving? Tall and scrawny, but he'd filled out. Hate had a way of doing that, maybe. Filling the empty places with something hard.

"That oil worker who had her things—her purse, her phone—he knew he couldn't be touched," Adam said. "You think we don't know those grunts can do anything on res land to our women and the law can't touch them? He walked, and your sheriff helped him. You helped him. And what did that big oil company do but move him out? He was gone to another state, another camp. But I found him."

Mark took in the cold, dark eyes staring back at him.

Adam's mouth barely moved when he spoke again. "He was in another camp in the Dakotas, where so many more sisters, daughters, and mothers have gone missing. Was it him or someone else? Doesn't matter. He'll never be found."

The chain on Adam's cuffs made a small sound as he shifted on the cot.

Mark stared at the man through the bars, knowing he'd hunted and killed him. "So that was my fate?" he said. "You made a list of everyone who did nothing, and you were coming after them? The sheriff, the deputies I worked with... What about the oil execs, the crew bosses on that pipeline who knew what he did? Maybe they were and still are part of it. What made me so special?"

The expression Adam shot him was something like a smile. "You remember what you said to my mother?"

He tried to remember, but all he could see in his mind was the anguish from a woman he'd have given anything to help.

"You said you wouldn't stop looking, that you'd find a way to get justice," Adam said, his voice flat. "That you'd find the man and see he was held accountable. You promised her. But it's the same lie that's been told to my people since the begin-ning of time."

Mark looked down at his hands, gripping the bars.

Dried blood caked under his nails.

Had he really said that? In his naivety, he'd believed the search for Whitney Chandler and her killer would be a priority. But the file cabinet was so full of cases that, as the deputy had said, they didn't have the time or resources for someone like her.

"When I got my badge and gun, I believed finding the bad guys and putting them away was all that mattered," Mark said, his voice raw. "I never could believe laws existed without a good reason. When the sheriff let Dwight Baker walk out that door... I'll never forget the smile on his face, the way he told the sheriff to go fuck himself. He told the deputy who picked him up that he'd be out before he walked through the doors of the station. Well, he did have to walk through the door, so he was wrong about that part. But the sheriff uncuffed him just inside and told him to go."

Adam's jaw tightened at the name.

Dwight Baker.

The name still alive in him. Still bleeding.

"I stood there in shock, furious, and demanded to know what the hell had just happened," Mark continued, the memory still vivid. "The sheriff told me to forget it. Said I had a nuisance call to look after, so I should get to it. I knew the deputy was pissed too. He told me later that the sheriff got a call from the company and was told to let Baker go or he'd have a serious problem. What had happened to that girl happened on res land. Baker was a redneck white asshole who worked the pipelines and knew what the hell he was doing. I was shuffled off to handle every shit call there was, but I spent hours on my own following up on your sister's case without telling the sheriff."

Adam's frown, the deep furrow in his brow, made Mark wonder if he believed him.

"I found a witness, a partial plate for the company truck that likely picked her up on the highway—and other girls too, I suspect. I learned from someone who used to work in the camp how girls would be brought in by the workers, or they would party out on res land at some isolated spot. Was your sister targeted?" He shook his head. He was sure it had been about the color of her skin. Easy prey.

"I think everyone who went missing was in the wrong place at the wrong time, and Dwight Baker didn't act alone. One of the crew bosses, a guy with a history of assaulting young women, sent a bottle of single-malt scotch as a gift to the sheriff. My mistake was reaching out to the Feds with the little I had, thinking they'd show up, take over the investigation with resources and agents, go after that camp, and put every asshole in there under a microscope because Indigenous women were being hunted and killed. There was enough evidence for them to do something, to look into it. But the sheriff called me into his office, sat me down, and suspended me for two weeks—a slap on the wrist because I overstepped. The Feds had reached out to him, questioning why a rookie deputy was using valuable resources on a no-win case..."

Adam turned to the concrete wall.

The small movement landed like a blow. For the first time since Mark had walked in, Adam looked away.

"And then you dropped it," Adam said, his voice quiet. The words were worse for it.

What was he supposed to say? He'd worked at that department for four years, a tenure that had ended in the very reason he was in Roche Harbor now.

"There were so many cases, I had to learn to pick my battles," Mark said. "I got into law enforcement to make a difference. I just didn't realize how deeply inequality is bred into the laws. A sheriff can pick and choose which laws he wants to enforce. Even the state governor has no authority over him. The state can order the state police to charge or investigate, but that's a call that doesn't happen. And sheriffs are elected for how long? There are laws that still need to be changed, ones that tie our hands. Let's be clear: The men in that camp knew exactly how it worked. You can't do what they did to a white girl from a good family and get away with it, but they could do it to your sister, to the other women on the reservation. I don't believe Dwight Baker acted alone. I think the company he worked for knew exactly what those men were doing, and they did nothing. They protected their asses by protecting them. And I think the sheriff knew all of it and looked the other way."

Adam only nodded, putting both feet on the floor. He sat up, resting his hand on his thigh, the chain between his cuffs sliding against denim.

Mark could see he hadn't expected this.

"You should never have promised my mother."

There was no anger in the words this time.

That was what made them cut deeper.

Mark pulled in a breath, knowing it was one of many mistakes he had made. He looked down at his boots, at the blood dried across the leather, and for a second he was back in that trailer, standing in front of a mother who wanted one person with a badge to tell her that her daughter mattered.

The door behind him opened.

Carmen stood there, one hand on the frame. The bandage on her forehead looked too white under the fluorescent lights.

"Mark," she said, her voice low. "Lawyer's here."

He turned back to Adam, who looked up at him and then away.

"Your dog going to be okay?" Adam asked.

"Don't know yet."

Adam only nodded.

Mark took a step away from the cell toward the door.

"I would have let her go after I shot you," Adam said.

Mark stopped.

The cell block went quiet again, except for the buzz overhead and the faint sound of Carmen breathing behind him.

He didn't look back.

He considered what Adam was saying for only a second. There was nothing he could say that wouldn't give Adam more than he deserved. No anger. No forgiveness. No absolution.

Nothing.

Mark walked out that door, and Carmen closed it behind him.

CHAPTER SEVENTEEN

"Hey, thanks for coming! So this is the famous Lucky?"

Billy Jo watched from the gray sectional, her feet up in socks, as Lesley fussed over Mark's dog. Mark walked slowly through the front door.

A truck door had slammed somewhere outside a minute earlier, and her fingers had tightened around the stem of her wineglass before she could stop herself. For one stupid second, she wasn't in Lesley's living room. She was back in that steel box, heat pressing down on her, cloth shoved in her mouth, rope burning her wrists, the sound of a bar sliding into place.

She'd told herself to breathe.

Then Lucky had limped through the door, slow and bandaged and very much alive, and she let out the breath she hadn't realized she was holding.

"Hi, Mark. Great that you could come," Chase said, reaching out to shake his hand. "You're Jed Friessen's son, right?"

It had been two days since Mark had shown up at the

metal cargo container and saved her. She'd seen a vulnerable side of him then, which was likely why they were back to the discomfort that lingered between them now.

"That's right, his youngest. My dad said your brother Vic is a good friend of my uncle's."

The pleasantries were out of the way, the familiarities. Then they were both looking at her.

"Billy Jo, can I refill your wine for you?" Lesley said as she strode in, barefoot, wearing black capris and a sleeveless dressy white blouse.

Billy Jo held up the empty glass. "I guess I'm not driving anywhere."

"Or walking far," Rose added, rising from the sofa. In faded blue jeans and a pink blouse, her blond hair shoulder-length, she was the kind of attractive woman Billy Jo knew she'd never be. Rose went straight to Mark. "Hi, Mark. Nice to see you again. Come in and sit."

Billy Jo patted Lucky's leg as the dog wandered over slowly, panting, a bandage still around his side. She knew Mark had just picked him up from the vet. She ran her hand over the dog's head.

"Mark, do you want a beer?" Lesley called from the kitchen, where Lorne was prepping steaks for the grill.

"Sure," Mark replied.

Billy Jo caught her mom's meaningful, teasing gaze—a clear reaction to Mark's presence. She looked away as Lesley strode in with her second glass of chilled white wine and a bottle of lager for Mark, who stood awkwardly.

"Thank you, Lesley," he said. "Not sure how long we can stay. I've got to get this guy home early."

Lesley simply waved a hand and patted his arm. "Nonsense. He looks quite comfortable, and dinner will be a while yet. Lorne is just getting the steaks prepped. Rose made apple pie for dessert. It will be nice to just have an evening of fun.

Come on and sit down. I'm going to see if Lorne needs a hand. Rose, Chase, you need a top-up?"

Billy Jo didn't catch her dad's response, but then both her mom and dad walked past the dining room and into the kitchen with Lesley. She watched them through the wide opening, listening to the laughter and the sound of more wine being poured. The radiating friendship between them wasn't lost on her.

"So, how are your feet?" Mark asked.

She wondered if she'd ever get the image out of her mind —him not wanting her to see him cry. That was a side the arrogant cop tried to hide.

"Sore," she said, letting sarcasm drip, her comfortable go-to personality. "Won't be running anywhere anytime soon. But wait, I hate running anyway, so..." She wasn't sure if he smiled as she leaned down, making herself look at the dog they had nearly lost, and ran her hand over him.

"So you really named him Lucky?" she asked. The dog looked up, lifted his head, and she noticed the slight wag of his tail.

"Seems perfect, considering."

She'd never seen this side of Mark—protective, worried. He really loved this dog. She didn't know how Lesley had convinced him to come for dinner, considering she'd only found out five minutes before he pulled in.

"So I heard Adam Chandler took a deal," she said.

Mark sat across from her in an easy chair, nursing his beer, his thumb working the label. It was the first time she'd seen him without his jean jacket. He wore a faded blue shirt, sleeves rolled up, revealing strong forearms.

He made a face, a silent nod, and for a moment, she wasn't sure he'd speak. Then he said, "He did. You okay with that?" His vibrant blue eyes met hers, but she felt a subtle distance between them.

She shrugged. "You asking if I expect you to lock him up and throw away the key?"

They could go back and forth like this, a familiar dance of words.

"Do you?" His voice was direct. He dangled the beer between his knees, then lifted it for a swallow, his gaze flicking toward the kitchen where the Lancasters and her parents were.

"Did he terrorize me? Sure. And yeah, I'm furious about how he did it, but so many things happened, Mark. More people aren't being held accountable. His sister was hunted, assaulted, murdered. But she was just one of many. This has been going on across the country for too long, and no one seems to care. Did he believe this was the only way to get justice? In fairness to him, it was. From talking to him, listening to him, I get it. I understand what drove him to that, but the ends don't justify the means.

"Then there's the call I got from that damn supervisor, nothing but a paper-pusher and a bureaucrat. He walked me right into that. Evidently, Adam knew how easy it would be, and no one is talking about where the report came from or how easy it was to send me out there. You know what really pisses me off? Not even an apology came down from Grant or from Lane Fuller, who I still haven't spoken to. My dad, the super lawyer, is super pissed and has already overstepped to read the riot act to Grant and his boss's boss, the head at the state level. Basically, he warned them their lives could become a living hell with the lawsuit he wants to bring down on them, because that's unfortunately the only way to fix their screwed-up system..."

There it was, the pull of his lips as he lifted the beer again, the rough laugh he tried to stifle. "Heard about that. New policy's coming down on Tuesday. Evidently, any call that comes in will require me, Carmen, or the chief to accompany you unless it's routine, whatever that means. They'll be looking at making it a policy across the state. So your dad is really suing?"

What was she supposed to say? Her dad couldn't stop himself. He'd always needed to fix everything, and his fear for her was why her parents were still here—in the Lancasters' guest room, thankfully, but still too close.

"He's basically got them under a microscope and will meet with state officials next week. He's still got a lot of political connections, and he's using them because of what happened. There's just so much about this he needs to change, that he *wants* to change. I can tell you the chief isn't exactly the person I want showing up on any doorstep with me, though."

She wondered if Mark had any idea how the chief had behaved when taking her statement. It was exactly as she'd expected. There had always been something about him, the way he talked to her. She wondered if he really saw her as his equal. It was that same feeling she'd grown up with, feeling so many look down on her, talk to her as if she were nobody. Of course, that made her unwilling to give him anything.

"He'll never win person of the year, but he's the chief."

She didn't know what to make of the edge in Mark's voice. "Cutting him some slack there, Mark?"

He didn't smile as he lifted the beer to his lips and swallowed. "You know, after what happened, it's had me looking at my entire career as a cop. Starting with my early years as a green, starry-eyed deputy, believing I could really do some good and make a difference. But I had no idea what I was suddenly part of, having to follow orders from a sheriff who could pick and choose who to charge for a crime, what to look away from, what laws to enforce for some and not others, which resources to use in an investigation, and which victims deserved cops showing up and actually giving a damn.

That naivety disappeared quickly when I saw how calls were handled and different people were treated—some respectfully, some with nothing. Then there were the kickbacks I suspected he received to look the other way. I'd like to say I've seen overreach, secrecy, and the kind of criminality in law enforcement I had no idea existed. It's dirty, but what's the answer? Because remember, while sheriffs like the chief are elected, they report to politicians with the kind of power over the little guy that has never sat right with me." Mark seemed to be in the dark, moody place she knew all too well.

"Well, that was a rather long-winded way of not really answering the question."

He flicked his gaze to the kitchen, then back to her, lifting a hand to rub his chin. "I'm not cutting anyone slack, but there's wisdom in sitting back and watching, listening, figuring out what's really going on, not tipping my hand too early."

"Okay, you two, dinner is almost ready," Lesley called out. "Lorne has the patio table set up outside, so why don't you bring your drinks out back?"

Mark stood. As Billy Jo put her feet on the ground, the dog slowly got up and followed, Lesley fussing over him. Mark held his hand out to her. She hesitated only a second before putting her hand in his, feeling the warmth, the grip that wouldn't let go. He helped her up.

"You want a piggyback?"

She didn't miss the edge of humor, the tug of his lips. She still held his hand, taking in the amusement that lingered for a second before she pulled her hand away. He offered his arm, and she slid her hand over it.

"Ha ha, funny. I can walk," she said, but she remembered his touch, his arms, the tension between them. She knew that other than her dad, he was the first guy to show up for her when things had gone sideways.

"But not run?" he said.

She made a rude noise as they strode into the kitchen, catching the teasing smiles, the way her mom and Lesley seemed overly interested in her and Mark. "Nope, not running for anyone," she said. She could hear the group fussing over the dog on the back deck.

He glanced down at her. "But you did run for Lucky, and for me."

Why did he have to point out that she cared?

As she held his arm, she felt him looking at her. "Yeah, well, don't go all sappy on me and let this go to your head. You showed up for me," she said. She made herself look up at him, feeling the discomfort in their closeness and the serious-ness in those vivid blue eyes that lingered on her.

"I'll always show up for you," he said.

There it was, that unease because someone really cared.

He looked away, his hand on her back as she went out the sliding glass door ahead of him, holding her glass of wine. She took in the empty chairs at the end, side by side, the only spots without drinks in front of them.

Evidently, her mom and Lesley had their own ideas about her and Mark.

CHAPTER EIGHTEEN

"WE DIDN'T GET A CHANCE TO TALK," CHASE MCCABE said, joining Mark on the manicured grass of the beautiful backyard. Mark stood, mug of coffee in hand, watching his dog sniff slowly across the lawn. He knew his vigilance showed, and appreciated that no one had teased him for it.

Chase was a tall man with light hair. Mark wondered if Billy Jo truly understood the depth of her parents' love. He'd seen it within five minutes of their arrival at the vet clinic, even in the way Chase had grilled him over the phone.

Mark nodded. Billy Jo, her mom, and Lesley were finishing a bottle of wine. He thought he'd heard Billy Jo laugh more tonight than ever before. "No, I guess not. Billy Jo mentioned you're causing a headache for DCFS."

Chase folded his arms across his chest. "It's a screwed-up system. Still can't believe she chose to work for it."

Mark wasn't sure what to make of the comment. "She wants to do right by those kids when no one else will, and she is."

Was that humor or a warning in her father's expression?

"And since I'm really stepping in it," Mark continued,

"you know the only way to fix something is to do something. She is, even though I can see her fighting a system that shows how incompetent it is."

Perhaps he should dial back his outrage, but he was still furious that two bureaucratic managers had effectively walked her into a situation where she could have ended up dead.

"Sounds like you're talking about yourself, too," Chase said. "Billy Jo told me about the problems you've had with the chief—not that she needed to, as I was there when he showed up to take her statement. Even though I want Adam Chandler locked up and the key thrown away, that won't solve anything. He's justifiably angry that most crimes against Indigenous people are rarely investigated, if at all. Most people don't get that. So what do you do when your sister or your mother or your daughter is assaulted, killed like his was? I know what I would do if it were Billy Jo. I wouldn't stop until every person who had turned a blind eye and hurt her was held accountable."

He hadn't expected that from her father, but then, there was something about a man who had taken in a kid like Billy Jo. He should have known Chase didn't and wouldn't fit into the mold, wouldn't sit back and look the other way.

"He likely killed the oil worker who did that to her," Mark said. "He admitted it to me. If I dig around, I wonder what I would find."

Chase McCabe didn't pull his gaze. "You going to report that?"

He didn't look away. "Report what?"

Silence stretched between them, broken only by the soft, easy laughter drifting from the patio—Billy Jo's voice mixed with Rose's and Lesley's. Lucky had stopped near the edge of the grass, nose down, moving slowly because of the bandage around his middle. Mark watched the dog for a second, then looked back at Chase.

Chase's expression had sharpened, telling Mark the man had heard what he hadn't said.

"One thing I learned in Washington," Chase said, "most men don't do the wrong thing because they wake up evil. They do it because standing up costs too much. Their job. Their pension. Their reputation. Their comfort. Sometimes their family."

Mark didn't answer.

The coffee mug in his hand grew cool. He thought of Whitney Chandler's file, Adam's mother. Dwight Baker walking out of the sheriff's office with a smile. He thought of Tolly, Gail's files, and every challenging look the chief gave him, daring him to ask the wrong question.

Chase looked at him. "So, what happens the next time it costs you?"

It wasn't a threat.

It was a test.

Mark dragged his gaze back to the deck, where Billy Jo sat with one foot tucked under her, laughing at something her mother said. He knew the laughter cost her, knew she was bruised and scraped, pretending she wasn't still hearing a metal bar slide into place.

"I don't know," he said.

Chase didn't blink.

Mark looked back at him. "But I know what happens if I look away."

Chase stared at him long and hard, then shifted his gaze to the dog. "You know what, Mark? I like you. But just to be clear, if you hurt my daughter, I will hunt you down and break you." He reached over and patted Mark's shoulder.

It took a moment for the words to sink in, for him to understand. Why did everyone keep assuming they were together?

"Got it," was all he said.

The dog wandered back over. Chase leaned down to rub him before looking back up.

"Good," he said. "Glad we had a chance to talk. Then there's your chief."

Mark glanced back to the women, still laughing. He wondered what else Billy Jo had said. "And what about him?"

Chase made a face. He could tell the man was about to fix everything. "I don't know, exactly, because I can't put my finger on it. But after all my years working in Washington with the players at the Capitol, I know there's always a game going on behind the scenes. What I knew the moment I walked into that station and met that chief was that he's playing the same kind of game."

Mark pulled in a breath, thinking of the files Gail had walked out with. It seemed the chief had his own way of doing things, and Mark wondered whether he'd ever have his back.

"Can't say for sure, but I'm watching," he finally said.

Chase nodded and gestured back to the deck, where the dog had wandered over to Billy Jo and lay down at her feet. "Good. If you find something..." he said in a low voice as they walked.

Mark shoved his hands in his pockets. "I'll call you and let you know."

EPILOGUE

MARK COULDN'T FIGURE OUT WHAT WAS DIFFERENT. THE chief was in his office, Gail was at her desk, and Carmen was on the phone, dealing with some complaint about a stolen lawnmower.

As he sat at his desk, listening to the phone ring, he took in Lucky, who was lapping fresh water from a steel bowl.

Gail answered the phone before he could reach for it. "Roche Harbor Police Department," she said, lifting her bag onto her desk. She pulled three files from it. "Who can I say is calling?" she asked, pressing the hold button and staring at him. She gestured as she settled the phone back into the cradle. "Fife Gattenburg, line two."

All Mark could do was stare at her, the name clicking into place. "You mean the California lawyer who owns the property where Billy Jo was locked up?"

She nodded. "The very same missing-in-action lawyer. Took his sweet time calling you, didn't he?"

Mark reached for the phone and pressed the line as Gail pulled open the filing cabinet behind her and tucked the files back inside. What the hell was she doing with them?

"Mr. Gattenburg, this is Detective Friessen. Took you only four days to call me back."

The man cleared his throat. "Sorry about that. Only just got the message. My secretary somehow overlooked giving it to me. It happens..."

Mark was familiar with assholes who blamed their secretaries.

"So what can I do for you, Detective?" Fife continued. "I understand from one of my tenants that you came by his place, asking for the name of my handyman."

Right, he'd probably already gotten his story lined up so he came out looking like the victim.

"I'm sure you've already heard that Adam Chandler was arrested for keeping a hostage in a metal cargo container on your property. Can you tell me how something like that was on your property and how long Mr. Chandler has been working for you?"

Fife cleared his throat again, a rustling sound in the background. "I'm sorry. As you probably understand, I own many properties and have limited knowledge of what goes on at each. I'm a California resident, so I hired a local to manage the property. I received my rent and never heard of any issues. Whatever Mr. Chandler was doing there was without my knowledge."

Mark held the phone, shaking his head. The man had said exactly what he'd expected.

"I trust Ms. McCabe is recovering," Fife said.

Mark stilled.

He hadn't used Billy Jo's name—not her first name, anyway. He'd said *hostage*. He'd said *Adam Chandler*. He'd said *cargo container*. Nothing more.

Across the room, Lucky lifted his head from the water bowl, his ears angling forward as if he'd picked up on Mark's shift before anyone else had.

"What did you say?" Mark asked.

"I said I trust Ms. McCabe is recovering," Fife replied smoothly. "A terrible ordeal, from what little I've heard."

What little I've heard.

Mark leaned back in his chair, feeling the scrape of old wood. "You seem pretty informed for a man who never got my message."

There was a small pause. Not long, just enough.

"It's a small island, Detective. News travels."

"Not to California that fast."

Fife gave a faint, humorless laugh. "You'd be surprised what reaches me when one of my properties is involved in a police matter. I also heard your dog was injured. Lucky, isn't it? Glad to hear he survived."

Mark didn't move.

Gail had stopped at the filing cabinet, her hand still on the drawer, but her eyes were on him now.

Lucky's name hadn't been in any report Mark had sent. Not yet. The vet knew. Gail knew. The station knew. Maybe half the island knew by now because people talked, but there was something about the way Fife said it, neat and polished, that crawled under Mark's skin.

"So how many properties do you own under...your shell company, is it?" Mark asked.

"Look, Detective, I'm not sure how that's relevant to this case."

"Oh, it's not. I'm just curious why someone owns that many properties."

He thought the man laughed. "Investments, is all. Now, again, I can't tell you anything about Mr. Chandler. A cargo container, you said? Well, I've never been to the property. It was most likely left there by the previous owner, or Adam Chandler moved it in. I expect it will be evidence you'll be moving off my property?"

"Why do you insist we clean the place up for you?"

"Right now, it's still a crime scene. We'll let you know when we're finished."

"Just out of curiosity, Detective, how did you find the container?"

Mark sat up straighter. "You mean because it was hidden in an outbuilding?"

"Well, Detective, I have to wonder if you had a warrant before going on my property."

He leaned forward, forearms on the desk, watching his dog. This man likely knew every loophole. What was this really about? "Mr. Gattenburg, your handyman, fired shots at me and my deputy. We discovered the container while trying to apprehend Adam Chandler. I'm not sure what this is. Do you have something to hide? Is there something you're not telling me?"

Mark's chair squeaked as he swiveled. Gail watched him, hearing only his side of the conversation.

"Just making sure you followed the letter of the law, Detective. As I said, I don't know Adam Chandler, just like all the caretakers I hire. I expect my investments to be managed, looked after, but I know nothing of their private lives or what goes on at the properties I own. As I said, they're investments. I've never been there. Is there anything else?"

Mark shook his head. "No, I guess not."

"Good day," Fife said before hanging up.

Mark held the phone, watching Gail pull two more files from her drawer and shove them into her bag. He stood, adjusting the waistband of his jeans as his dog wandered to the dog bed and lay down.

"He gave you the runaround, didn't he?" Gail asked.

Mark walked to her desk, noting the files sticking out of her bag. One label read "Brown," the other "Jefferson." "He basically told me he knows nothing about the caretaker he hired and has never been to the property because it's just an investment. Oh, and when I asked him about the number of properties he owns under his shell corporation, he didn't answer."

Gail's lips twitched, her gaze sharpening. "That's not all he said."

Mark rested his hands on the edge of her desk. "No. He knew Billy Jo's name. He knew Lucky had been shot."

Gail was silent for a second.

From the chief's office, Tolly's low voice carried through the closed door, but Mark couldn't make out the words. Carmen was still on the phone, one hand over her ear, not paying attention—or pretending not to.

Gail slowly set her hand on top of the files in her bag. "Did you tell him either of those things?"

"No."

Her expression flickered, a momentary change, then was gone.

"Then maybe Mr. Gattenburg listens better than he talks," she said.

He shrugged. "Yeah. I mean, why own all that, and for what?"

She rested her hands on her bag. "Money, Mark. It's always about money. Real estate is a great investment, and Mr. Gattenburg owns close to eighty properties worldwide. Quite the nest egg he's amassing."

He didn't know what to say. He gestured to her bag. "I meant to ask what you're doing with the files, taking them home. Working on something?"

She only smiled, reaching for her keys in her drawer. "Someone has to keep these files neat and tidy. So, I'm off. You man the phones; Carmen has to head out on rounds. And you should bring Billy Jo over for dinner sometime."

She pulled her sunglasses from her bag, resting them on her head as she looped the bag over her shoulder. At the door, she paused, looking back at him. "You know, we all see you have feelings for her, and she for you. Just ask her out already. And I mean it about dinner. Say, Friday?" She waited for his answer.

"I'll have to talk to her. She might be busy."

Gail laughed. "You do that, Mark. You do that."

Then she stepped out. He watched the closed door, then glanced at the chief on the phone in his office. Deciding not to overthink it, he reached for the phone and dialed Billy Jo's number.

"DCFS. This is Billy Jo."

"Hey, it's Mark. Listen, are you doing anything Friday?"

A moment of silence. "Why?"

He let the receiver slide from his mouth, a soft laugh escaping him. "We've been invited for dinner at the chief's."

She said nothing, but he heard her sigh.

"Is that a yes?" he asked, a suspicion forming that she might just as easily say no.

"Fine. But, Mark, this isn't a date."

He couldn't fight the twitch of a smile, glad she couldn't see it. "Absolutely not a date. I'll pick you up at six."

She hesitated a second. "Don't be late." Then she hung up.

He settled the phone in its cradle and murmured under his breath, "I won't, Billy Jo. I definitely won't be late, not for you."

TURNING POINT

NEXT IN THE BILLY JO MCCABE MYSTERY

His crime was unforgivable, but the law protects him.

If an alleged crime is reported to you, but no victim can be found, has a crime been committed? This is exactly the question Billy Jo McCabe asks Detective Mark Friessen when an anonymous woman approaches her and tells her about an unspeakable crime taking place right under the watch of the chief of police, in his own family.

When Billy Jo reaches out to Mark with the story, he just can't look away. They soon learn family is family, and the victim has been hiding her secret for years. But she's not just any victim: She's Cheyenne Potter, the niece of the chief of police, Tolly Shepard.

Mark has always suspected Tolly is a man of many secrets. Because he just can't sit by, he partners up with Billy Jo to dig into the chief, his family, and the secret they're hiding. He's convinced the chief helped bury a crime, but every answer they find only exposes another question. The players in this game are people who use the law to their advantage, and even though neither Mark nor Billy Jo is afraid of a fight, they soon learn that stepping on the wrong toes may lead them into a fight they can't win. Sometimes the law doesn't protect the innocent—and it has the best nondisclosures money can buy.

"You ready to go?" Mark called out the minute he stepped into her place.

No "Hi." No "How are you?" It was always "Hurry up, already."

Billy Jo stared at the makeup she'd been about to put on, then tossed it back in her makeup bag, untouched. What had she been thinking, forking over her hard-earned cash on a whim for something she never wore?

"Seriously, Billy Jo, what are you doing?" she said to her reflection in the mirror as she flicked her hands through her plain and boring shoulder-length brown hair, noting the freckles that dotted her nose.

She'd never be the supermodel type. So, again, why was she doing this?

"Hey, didn't you hear me? What are you doing in here?" Mark said as he strolled in.

She stared up at the tall, rugged, arrogant cowboy. His new jean jacket didn't quite match his faded blue jeans, and his wavy red hair was short and appeared freshly cut. The way he talked to her, it was always as if he didn't have a clue what she was thinking. He rested his hand on the doorframe and took in her small bathroom.

"I'm doing what a girl does: getting ready," she said. "You said dinner at that new Mexican place. You made a reservation?"

He stepped back from the doorway, dragging his gaze down, taking in her new sleeveless black blouse and dressy capris, a gift from her mom. He had her feeling both uncomfortable and awkward.

"What?" She knew it came out quite sharply.

There was the pull of his lips, the smile that wasn't really a smile but rather a sign of his amusement at her expense. Maybe that was why she could feel the frown knitting her brow.

"Didn't say anything," he said. "And no, didn't get around to making a reservation. We don't need it."

She wondered at times what it was about him that had her wanting to pull her hair out. "It's new and it's busy. We need a reservation or it's going to be fish tacos at the stand again—and I'd rather not, if it's all the same to you."

He only angled his head, those blue eyes flickering, too good to look at. She knew he would rather argue than just go along with what he was supposed to do. But that seemed to be who they were and how this thing, whatever this was between them, worked.

"You worry too much," he said.

At the jab, she felt her hands fisting at her sides. "And you seem to think we can just walk right in there and...what, we'll be given a table?"

He flicked his jacket back as if trying to make a point, resting his hand right beside his badge, tucked into the waistband of his jeans. He said nothing.

"You seriously think you can just show your badge and they'll bump us right to the front of the line?" she said.

He made a rude noise, one she'd heard from him too many times when she just didn't go along with his way of thinking. "You make it sound like a bad thing. Everyone knows who I am…"

She could tell exactly what he'd been thinking by the way he trailed off. "And you don't think there's anything wrong with that? Walking right in, past all the people who actually thought ahead to make reservations, past anyone else waiting their turn on the list? You seriously think that just because you're a cop here, you get priority?" She flicked off the light in the bathroom and stepped out.

He suddenly seemed at a loss for words. "Now, wait a second. That wasn't what I meant."

She angled her head. He stepped back, and she walked around him to the island, where her cell phone was plugged in and charging. She took a second to check that it was in the green, at one hundred percent. As she looked over, she thought he dropped an F-bomb under his breath before pulling his cell phone from his pocket and dialing.

"Yeah, this is Detective Mark Friessen. This is probably short notice, but do you have a table available for dinner for two? I was planning on coming now and just showing up, but it was pointed out to me that you're likely busy, and…"

She could hear someone talking on the other end.

"Uh-huh," was all Mark said. As he flicked his gaze over to her, his blue eyes seemed to simmer with something. "Sounds great. We're on our way," he said, then hung up and tucked his phone in his pocket.

She stared at what seemed to be smugness in his expression.

"Apparently there's always a table available for me," he said. Then he shrugged. "I called like you said. You should be happy now." He gestured as if she'd made a big deal out of nothing.

"Yet you just couldn't help yourself from using your detective title before asking for a table," she said. "Mark, it's the same as if you'd walked in there and flashed your badge. Ever heard of abuse of authority? There shouldn't always be a table for you. That is very much someone giving you something for a favor." She tucked her phone in her bag.

He narrowed his gaze. "I am the last person to use my position to get something. Seriously, I don't work that way. I can't be bought and don't give out special favors. You're making it sound as if I'm taking a kickback or something. I pay my own way. I don't take gifts or bribes."

She pulled her arms over her chest, taking in how defensive he suddenly sounded. "I hate to tell you this, but a table in a crowded restaurant is a kickback, whatever you want to call it, if you got it using your position in the community."

"Do you want me to cancel? Is that what this is?"

She realized in that second that he didn't get it. He stared at her with what she thought was the usual frustration that happened in their discussions, where she had one idea and he seemed to pull counterarguments from his ass.

"No, I'm hungry," she said. "Let's go."

He stood there for a second as if he didn't believe her. "There's a test in here, right?"

She didn't smile. She didn't say anything. She simply took in her three-legged cat, Harley, as he hopped up onto the sofa. Mark looked down at her with the same kind of apprehension with which he might have looked at a ticking timebomb.

"Don't look so worried," she finally said. "Let's go. But hear me on this: If we get there and there's a crowd waiting, and, sure enough, they've bumped you to the front of the line because of your phone call, you say no to the table and ask them to put us in the queue, where we should have been to begin with."

He lifted his hands as if surrendering. "Fine. Point made," he said, then gestured to the door.

Billy Jo had to remind herself that it wasn't healthy to enjoy this butting of heads that seemed to come naturally between her and Mark.

ABOUT THE AUTHOR

Lorhainne Eckhart, a New York Times & USA Today best-selling author, crafts stories of undeniable intimacy and family drama, earning her the title of "Queen of the family saga." Her works delve deep into the complexities of family dynamics, mingling suspense and angst with a touch of romance to engage readers on multiple levels. Renowned for her 'Raw Relatable Real Romance,' Lorhainne's narratives reflect strong moral themes and the importance of family.

With over 145 titles across multiple series now available in Italian, Spanish, French, and German, Lorhainne continues to captivate a global audience. Her literary contributions have garnered multiple Readers' Favorite Awards for Suspense and Romance. Beyond her writing, she is a mother of three, an advocate for autism awareness, and a believer in pursuing dreams.

Stay updated on her latest releases and promotional offers by following Lorhainne on Bookbub and subscribing to her mailing list at <u>LorhainneEckhart.com</u>, where you can also find her Monday Blog on all things books and life.

"Lorhainne Eckhart has this uncanny way of just hitting the spot every time with her books."

— (CAROLINE L., REVIEWER)

Lorhainne loves to hear from her readers! You can connect with me at:
www.LorhainneEckhart.com
lorhainneeckhart.le@gmail.com

facebook.com/AuthorLorhainneEckhart
x.com/LEckhart
instagram.com/lorhainneeckhart
bookbub.com/profile/lorhainne-eckhart
pinterest.com/lorhainneeckhart

SERIES AVAILABLE

Billy Jo McCabe Mystery: The social worker and the cop, an unlikely couple drawn together on a small, secluded Pacific Northwest island where nothing is as it seems

The Dating Deception Series is a clean romantic suspense thriller series about love, lies, and the dangerous side of modern dating. Each book follows a different betrayal—romance scams, catfishing, manipulated matches, love bombing, false identities, and deadly secrets—where trust is weaponized, hearts are targeted, and survival means finding the courage to reclaim your voice.

The Watchers: Six unlikely friends, with a diverse set of skills, are brought together to face off against a common enemy in the mind-bending new series The Watchers.

The Friessen Legacy: Embrace heartwarming Friessen family love across three series, *The Outsider, The Friessens: A New Beginning and The Friessens*

The McCabe Brothers: Join the five McCabe siblings on their journeys to the dark and dangerous side of love.

The O'Connells: Journey into Love and Danger with the unconventional O'Connells of Montana

The Parker Sisters: Small-Town Love and sisterly bonds: Join the Parker Sisters of Wyoming on their heartfelt journey to finding Love

The Street Fighter: Welcome to the gripping world of the Streetfighter mystery series where justice is a battle fought on the mean streets and in the corridors of power

The Wilde Brothers: Enter the world of the Wilde Brothers a captivating Idaho family saga of romance rugged charm and strong bonds.

Walk the Right Road: Featuring a faked death, a dangerous choice and more, this stunning series of love and suspense will take you on an irresistible journey

The Saved Series: Love, danger and survival: Join Abby and Eric for a riveting journey of heart-pounding romance and suspense

Kate & Walker: Dive into a suspenseful romance series with Kate & Walker.

Married in Montana: Discover Heartfelt Romance and Second Chances in the Married in Montana Series

In the Charm
Unexpected Consequences
It Was Always You
The First Time I Saw You
Welcome to My Arms
Welcome to Boston
I'll Always Love You
Ground Rules
A Reason to Breathe
You Are My Everything
Anything For You
The Homecoming
Stay Away From My Daughter
The Bad Boy
A Place of Our Own
The Visitor
All About Devon
Long Past Dawn
How to Heal a Heart
Keep Me In Your Heart

The O'Connells
The Neighbor
The Third Call
The Secret Husband
The Quiet Day
The Commitment
The Missing Father
The Hometown Hero
Justice
The Family Secret
The Fallen O'Connell
The Return of the O'Connells
And The She Was Gone

The Stalker
The O'Connell Family Christmas
The Girl Next Door
Broken Promises
The Gatekeeper
The Hunted

The Dating Deception Series
Lured by Lies
Profile of a Stranger
The Perfect Match
Love Bombed

The McCabe Brothers
Don't Stop Me (Vic)
Don't Catch Me (Chase)
Don't Run From Me (Aaron)
Don't Hide From Me (Luc)
Don't Leave Me (Claudia)
Out of Time

A Billy Jo McCabe Mystery
Nothing As it Seems
Hiding in Plain Sight
The Cold Case
The Trap
Above the Law
The Stranger at the Door
The Children
The Last Stand
The Charity
The Sacrifice

The Street Fighter

Finding Home
Finding Honor
Finding Redemption

The Wilde Brothers
The One (Joe and Margaret)
The Honeymoon, A Wilde Brothers Short
Friendly Fire (Logan and Julia)
Not Quite Married, A Wilde Brothers Short
A Matter of Trust (Ben and Carrie)
The Reckoning, A Wilde Brothers Christmas
Traded (Jake)
Unforgiven (Samuel)
The Holiday Bride

Married in Montana
His Promise
Love's Promise
A Promise of Forever

The Parker Sisters
Thrill of the Chase
The Dating Game
Play Hard to Get
What We Can't Have
Go Your Own Way
A June Wedding

Kate & Walker
One Night
Edge of Night
Last Night

Walk the Right Road Series

The Choice
Lost and Found
Merkaba
Bounty
Blown Away: The Final Chapter
He Came Back

The Saved Series
Saved
Vanished
Captured

Single Titles
Loving Christine